Calling
NURSE BLAIR

Lucy Agnes Hancock

WILDSIDE PRESS

CHAPTER ONE

VISITING HOURS were over for the day and Haddon Memorial Hospital was settling down. Alex Blair, one of the night nurses, put down the chart on which she had been working and closed her eyes for a moment. Faintly from across the city, the notes of Saint Mark's carillon came to her soothingly. She murmured the prayer in her heart.

> *"Oh Lord, our God*
> *Be Thou our Guide,*
> *That by Thy help*
> *No foot may slide."*

"Nine o'clock," Bailey said superfluously, joining her a moment later. "The Lyons gal in 511 quarreled with her boy friend and sent him packing early and now she wants him back. I told her nothing doing until morning. It would serve her right if he refused to come back. That girl has the worst disposition I ever came across, Blair. She's pretty, too, and charming when she wants to be. She begged me to telephone him that she was sorry. Imagine! I won't, but I thought you might. Will you? Here's his number."

Alex laughed softly at the other's reluctance to appear anything but quite matter-of-fact and impersonally professional.

"The girl's sick, Bailey," she chided.

"That's no excuse, Blair. She's spoiled."

Alex reached for the telephone extension on the desk. The young man who answered begged to come back at once, but Alex told him it would be better to wait until morning; after ten. She was smiling when she replaced the instrument, and Bailey said that instead of Alex her name should be Miss Fixit. She went to relay the message, however, although not affably. 511 needed a bit of discipline. Do her good.

A light bloomed above the door of 517 and Alex moved silently down the long corridor. In the narrow hospital bed, the patient lay tense and unhappy. Alex's gray eyes were sympathetic.

"This bad time will pass, Mrs. Peterson," she said soothingly as she adjusted the bed to the desired angle.

"I know how uncomfortable you are. But the worst is definitely over and from now on you will improve steadily. I know, you see, because I have taken care of several thyroid cases—some of them much worse than yours. Won't you try to relax, rest, and perhaps sleep? Tomorrow will be better I promise you." She smoothed the coverlet over the elderly patient and smiled down at her. "Very soon now, you will be thankful that you submitted to that operation when you did. You will forget the pain and discomfort in the added feeling of well-being. If you want me for anything just put on the light. I shall be right here." The nurse's voice was quiet and soothing and very comforting, and the patient managed a smile of gratitude.

Out in the long, dim corridor a trio of nurses talked in low voices, and as Alex approached one of them walked away toward the elevator. The others turned to smile at her.

"That one needs to have her head examined," Bailey said derisively. "Guess what she came over here to tell us, Blair."

Alex shook her head. "I haven't a notion."

"That the Chief's granddaughter thinks Halliday *passe*; that she is too strict. Also that she's after the new assistant—Ellen Ridley, I mean is after him. Oh, pardon me, Blair," she grinned in mock distress, "I forgot that you don't approve of gossip."

Alex laughed. "Don't make me out a prig, Bailey," she chided, "although I confess I try to avoid gossip when I can."

"I know," the older nurse agreed, "but just the same we do need a bit of spice in our conversation occasionally just to keep us from getting stale. And believe me, Doctor Allen will provide us with plenty if what Olsen says is true. Anyway, it will be a change from the constant talk of Ridley as a misplaced night superintendent. I'm sure sick of that subject. What do you think of Doctor Allen, Blair?"

"Why, I don't know," Alex answered. "I haven't had anything to do with him; haven't happened to come in contact with him, Bailey. Why?"

"I asked first," Bailey smiled. "You've seen him haven't you? Hasn't he tried to date you yet?"

4

Alex Blair shook her head vigorously. "Don't be silly, Bailey. He wouldn't dare."

"Dare? But why not? He's a member of the staff. A ranking member at that. I bet he would dare—"

"Don't talk nonsense," Alex answered, and slipped away to answer a light suddenly blooming above the door of 512. Samuel Phillips was convalescing from an embolism in his right leg. He had been a patient in Haddon Memorial for nearly six months. It had been a long, trying time of almost complete inaction. But the results were gratifying. The clot had been dissolved, the hot saline compresses discontinued and, except for a quite natural but temporary weakness, the leg was sound as before. But Doctor Hammond was not quite ready to discharge the patient who was past middle-age and inclined to be over active.

Samuel Phillips was an important man. A week longer under the watchful eye of nurses was time well spent and the resident of Haddon Memorial was determined to see that his orders were obeyed in spite of the fact that the patient was daily becoming more impatient. Alex pushed open the door and went in.

"Did you want something, Mr. Phillips?" she asked.

"Nothing that I'm apt to get," the patient answered morosely. "I'm bored—simply bored. Why can't I go home tonight; right now? I'm perfectly well, or as well as I'm ever likely to be," he went on. "Get hold of Hammond, Nurse. Tell him I insist on getting out of here at once."

Alex's smile was almost maternal as she shook her head at the impatient man. "And do you think Doctor Hammond will let you leave at once, Mr. Phillips?" she chided.

"He will if I make enough fuss," the patient said slyly. "I have been an exemplary patient, I heard you tell the supervisor so just last night. But I am quite capable of making a scene, you know."

"I haven't a doubt about it," Alex assured him, "only I feel sure you won't. You see, Mr. Phillips, I know you are a reasonable man. We here at Haddon have found you cooperative and appreciative of what the hospital has done and is still doing for you, and so I am not at all worried about your making a scene and getting us into trouble."

"Getting you into trouble, Nurse?" the man said

5

quickly. "Of course I wouldn't think of doing anything of the kind. It is only that—oh, you just wouldn't understand."

"But I do," the nurse told him. "I understand perfectly and I shall give you an alcohol rub, and bring you a glass of warm milk, and then you are going to relax and think of the pleasantest thing that ever happened to you. How is that for an interesting program?"

The man grinned at her. "You are very convincing, Nurse," he said. "And do you think that leg will be all right in time?"

"It is all right now. Of course you are leg conscious. You favor it, and it tires easily. But remember that it has been inactive for quite a time and has grown lazy. But in another month or so you will forget all about it and you will find yourself using it as naturally as you do the other. Now I shall give you that rub, and then for the milk."

The man said nothing more except to tell her it felt good as she rubbed the tired back, and his grin was boyish as he murmured, "I'm sorry to be such a nuisance, Nurse."

Alex smiled down at him. The strained look had left his face and after a moment she slipped from the room. Once again she had averted a period of low spirits. Somehow she had discovered that very often convalescents succumbed to blue spells, especially when experiencing a touch of homesickness or fear. Samuel Phillips had been a frightened man when he arrived at Haddon some months ago, and it required every trick Alex and the resident knew to dissipate that panic. Now as she watched him sip the warm milk and heard his sigh of relaxation as he slipped lower in the bed, she felt an upsurge of pleasure and of accomplishment. She closed the door and walked to the desk in the alcove just now vacant. If there came times when she longed for the happy carefree days of her childhood, she refused to dwell on them for long or on the dark days succeeding the tragedy that had made her a serious-minded woman before the years warranted. Nursing was to be her lifework.

Was it only five years ago that she, the then popular Lisa Blair was considered a real menace to the group of girls of which she was reputed to be the leader? They used to tell her she could have any man in town, and to prove them right she had chosen the one considered the most eligible, no doubt to the relief yet possible envy of the others. How vividly it all came back to her!

Philip Matson was the only son of the wealthy suburbs foremost citizen. The Matsons not only had wealth but prided themselves on having a lineage that was above reproach—an escutcheon without spot or blemish. The two elder Matson girls had married into families almost as flawless as their own, and the only son was on the verge of making a satisfactory marriage with the lovely and desirable Lisa Blair whose paternal grandfather had, on the death of an elder brother, refused an English title, preferring to remain plain Zachariah Blair of Blair Acres. And then had come the tragedy that had shaken the conservative suburb to its foundations and had brought about the death of stanch old Zachariah. He was proud of his handsome grandson, Lisa's brother Peter, and spoiled him from the day the boy had come to live with him. He had paid his bills, overlooked his college scrapes, his dismissal from Law School because of continued misdeeds—excusing them all as merely the result of pure animal spirits. It had been a great satisfaction when at twenty the boy enlisted as a private, refusing to even consider officers' training. That was true to the Blair tradition. Zachariah was deaf to whispered scandal— hints of forged checks, of misappropriation of funds, of evil companions, even of a midnight elopement and a wedding before a Justice of the Peace in a neighboring town. And then had come the night when after a riotous party the boy had shot and killed his bride of a few hours and, whether in remorse or actual fear, had shot himself. With this final act came disclosure of all the rest, and the old man's stout heart broke.

Eighteen-year-old Lisa was stunned by the double loss—that of her beloved grandfather who had been mother and father to her since early childhood, and the death of her adored brother under circumstances at once tragic and disgraceful. The double funeral was private— only a few of her scattered kin, none closely related, attending more in curiosity than actual sorrow, for there was little love between them and the master of Blair Acres. They had nothing to gain. There was little left, and at the

7

girl's refusal to accept their reluctant invitations to share their homes for a time, they forthwith departed and Lisa was left alone.

Lawyers came—men who had handled the legal affairs of the Blairs in good times and evil—and they found things in bad shape. There was but little money, a few thousand dollars perhaps, and Blair Acres, her home for most of her life, must go. And Lisa, gazing about the old house dry-eyed, wept inwardly.

They asked about her plans. They were concerned. Lisa was a young and lovely girl. And Lisa told them she would find employment, although she had no training for work. She could be a charming hostess. She could dance, play tennis, ride a horse, drive a car, play a satisfactory game of bridge. She could wear expensive clothes and had, on occasion, acted in Little Theater Productions, but, as she confided to the family doctor when he inquired as to her future plans, none of her talents were marketable.

The doctor had heard, as everyone had heard or surmised, that her engagement to the eligible Philip Matson had been broken. Why or how was Lisa's own secret. She reviewed the affair bitterly. Oh, Phil had been kind, sympathetic, even chivalrous wanting to marry her at once and leave town, go far away where no one would know of the disgrace, where they could begin life together without the stigma which, locally, would forever cling to the Blair name. Lisa had listened stonily. Frozen for a moment, then burning with anger, she had snatched the ·ring from her finger and handed it to him without a word. She had seen the relief with which he had accepted it, and she had opened the door wide for him to leave without even a good-bye. She had been far too hurt for tears and thereafter had left orders to old Sarah Thompkins, the sole retainer who had refused to leave with the other servants, that no one else was to be admitted. She had no desire to see anyone. She wanted no one's pity. She wasn't old Zachariah Blair's granddaughter for nothing. She wasn't licked yet. She would show them!

And so when Doctor Whitcomb suggested that she go to a sister of his who had a sort of rest house in the mountains, the girl was glad to get away, exacting a promise from the doctor that he tell no one of her whereabouts. It was while there that she decided to become a nurse, partly because her hostess had been and still was a nurse and partly because it seemed to fit her mood. She wanted work. She needed hard work. Work that would make her forget the past and the people who once had made up her life. She entered the training school at the small but efficient Memorial Hospital at Haddon, and she found the duties hard and exacting and was grateful. She must keep hands and mind occupied so there would be no time to think.

And although she still missed her old home and the friends of her girlhood, she refused to dwell upon that loss. She refused to look back, but lived each day as it came, determined to let the future take care of itself. She made but few friends and was considered by her associates to be proud and exclusive. The days, months and years went by at snail's pace and then suddenly one bright June day she stood with some dozen student nurses to receive her diploma and the pin that proclaimed to the world that she had passed the test and was now a graduate nurse. Almost at once the State awarded her the degree of R.N. and Alexandra Elizabeth Blair was ready to face the world. Most of her class not entering the holy bonds of matrimony left Haddon to take up private work, but Lisa remained at the hospital as a general duty nurse, doing excellent work and admired by management and patients alike.

Alex loved the hospital. The building was old and not too modern, at least the original tall, six storied building was not. It towered above the newer wings, seeming to dominate not only the rest of the hospital but the countryside as well. There had been no attempt on the part of construction engineers engaged to modernize and increase the size of the hospital, to follow the original plan of using bricks for the work, and the new part, much the larger, was constructed of cement blocks to a height of merely four stories. Consequently Haddon Memorial Hospital had something the appearance of a mongrel, and yet management and staff were proud of it and intensely loyal to it.

The Chief of Staff, Doctor Felix Mathews, was one of the best brain surgeons in the country, and was not only honored but beloved by all who knew him. The city of Haddon itself was like a big country town rambling over several miles of lovely countryside. It was located on one of the State's most beautiful lakes and boasted two hospitals, many churches, excellent schools and a junior college of national repute. The streets were wide, well paved and tree bordered with well kept homes and spacious lawns of which the towns-people were justly proud, as they were of the fine parks and wide boulevard extending from the center of the city to the picturesque lake in the suburbs. A delightful city of homes, but far removed from being a hustling metropolis. Haddon contained but few millionaires—several wealthy families to be sure, but none immensely so. It impressed one as being a very livable, leisurely, homey and desirable town, desirable for those who had acquired a competence and wanted nothing more from life than to live simply and to enjoy the fruits of their labors. Some of the young people complained that it was dead, that there was nothing doing, no future for them, and many drifted away to greener more exciting fields in larger cities.

Lisa, however, fell in love with Haddon on her first sight of the place and felt that here she could begin life anew—a stranger in a strange city. Sponsored by Mrs. Bigelow, she felt sure that no one here was apt to connect her with the recent tragic events of the upstate Blairs. Not that she felt shame. Her grandfather was above reproach. And Pete? Peter had never really grown up. He had been adored and spoiled by everyone. He was reckless, thoughtless—a daredevil, but not bad. Never bad. The forged checks, the stories of theft, the marriage to the girl from across the river that culminated in murder and suicide? There was some explanation—there must be for her adored brother, so sweet and dear, was not a bad boy. But Lisa Blair had not yet reached the stage where she could discuss the affair objectively. She wanted no connection with the past. And here she was known as Alex Blair, making use for the first time in her life of the detested Alexandra. She had signed her full name to her application—Alexandra Elizabeth Blair—and was thereafter known as Alex Blair. She didn't like it, but at least it was different from the Lisa of happier days.

Sometimes she wondered what the old crowd might be doing—who was married to whom and if there were any children. Where this and that one might be living, and if the beloved home, Blair Acres, was sold and who the new owners were. Some day, perhaps when she was old, she would go back to Valary incognito just to look at the place and to dream. But that would be in the far distant future when the wound should have healed and time had woven a veil of forgetfulness across the tragic past.

There had been occasions during her three years of training when she had dreaded the possibility of someone from Valary being brought into the hospital, but with the passing of time that fear had disappeared. Haddon was a long way—half across the state—from Valary, and some of the ice around her heart had melted and she no longer experienced a thrill of fear each time she was assigned to a new case. Still she could not bring herself to let down the bars of her aloofness. She was pleasant to the other nurses, but inclined to be reserved and even cool to the doctors. She was, perhaps, easier with the Chief of Staff than with anyone else, and he in turn seemed to admire her. Of course this brought on the complaint of favoritism and of apple polishing, but the girl didn't care. She seemed not to resent criticism for the simple reason that she failed to accept it. She was there to work, to care for the sick, and to obey the strict rules and schedules, and nothing else really mattered to her.

With Marie Halliday, the superintendent, she was a favorite but solely because of her willingness to do anything she was asked to do, often adding further time to the already long ten hours which was the work period permitted at Haddon Memorial. She never complained, never broke rules, never gossiped about her patients, and was one of the few nurses who had no fault to find with the food served. An ideal nurse, Miss Halliday contended. A girl in a thousand, Doctor Mathews pronounced. A human iceberg, the younger doctors stated—but oh, how lovely! And Alex Blair appeared oblivious of their attitudes, their criticism, or their admiration.

Patients adored Alex Blair and left the hospital loud in her praise. Somehow life seemed brighter, more worthwhile to them after a few days in the care of the quiet, lovely girl with the steady gray eyes and bright hair. Her soft mobile lips were never severe although laughter was by no means common to them. Her smile was a lovely thing, and sometimes her patients strove to bring one to her rather sad face.

"I don't think your name suits you at all, Nurse," one of the doctors told her after she had helped him adjust the cast on an old lady's broken leg.

"No?"

"Alex. Probably short for Alexandra. Too stiff, too stodgy for you. You should be Diana, Chloe, or even Judith."

"But no one here calls me Alex, Doctor," she reminded him evenly. "I am Blair."

"I know. A horrid custom. But at that I like it better than your name. Somehow Blair suits you. One can quite easily see you, hair flying, eyes aglow, a tennis racket in your hand as you make a mad dash for the ball. Or even picture you riding along a narrow trail with the wind in your face. Why, you might even be dancing, slim and lovely in filmy white in the arms of some handsome young Lochinvar. Why are you here nursing the sick, my dear?" he asked whimsically.

Alex had stiffened as he began speaking; then gradually she had relaxed. The man meant nothing rude or unkind. She sensed that. He was one of the town's leading physicians, a middle-aged man who but recently had lost an only daughter.

"You sound like a romanticist, Doctor Widmer," she told him. "I am here because I like nursing, taking care of the sick. I hope I am a good nurse. The life you picture is probably attractive to those enjoying it, but the one I live here is very worthwhile."

"I know," the man answered. "I know. There, Mrs. Roberts, isn't that better? Of course it is. You'll be all right now. Just take it easy and enjoy your stay with us. Let me know if there is anything I can do. I must stop in and tell that granddaughter of yours that you aren't going to die this time."

He laughed and winked at the nurse, while the patient surprised Alex by making a little face at him.

12

CHAPTER TWO

BUT THAT SUN room is unheated, Mordock," young Doctor Allen pointed out somewhat curtly. He was tired. The operation had been a difficult emergency appendectomy, and he was anxious to get his patient settled for the night.

"It is the only vacancy we have on this floor, Doctor," the supervisor stated firmly. "The only one in the entire hospital I have no doubt. Your patient will have to have the sun room." Her blue eyes were cool, and she met the surgeon's look of antagonism calmly. She was within her rights and she knew it. This young surgeon was too big for his britches and needed taking down a peg. Who did he think he was to come in here and give orders questioning the management of the floor?

"It is quite unthinkable," the young man said, his jaw appearing to jut out and his dark eyes smoldering angrily.

The supervisor shrugged and turned to the desk before which she was working. The surgeon stalked down the corridor. He hesitated before the door of 315. Bill Andrews was about ready to go home. He was practically well. Doctor Allen went in. The patient in warm robe and slippers was sitting beside the window watching the lights of the city below. He turned as his door opened.

"Oh, hello, Doctor!" he greeted the newcomer. "Making good night calls? Well, this will be your last for me. I shall be glad to be home, Doc, even if you have all been very kind to me." He stretched his arms above his head and sighed deeply. "It's good to be able to do that again. Sort of rests one, doesn't it?"

Doctor Allen smiled for a moment, then he sobered. "I have a favor to ask of you, Bill," he began. "I know you aren't to be discharged until tomorrow morning, but I'm wondering if you would be willing to give up this room tonight, right now, and take the unheated sun room down the hall. I will help you move your things and will order extra blankets and perhaps even manage an electric heater. What do you say?"

He watched the man before him narrowly. Bill Andrews boasted that no one ever pushed him around. He paid for what he got and demanded value received. This room was one of the best and most expensive in the hospital, but he had not quibbled at the price nor at the treatment of nurses and doctors. Now he frowned slightly, and Doctor Allen went on to explain.

"You see, I have just performed an emergency on a young woman—a rather serious one—and the only vacancy in the entire place is a bed in the unheated sun room. I'm sure you understand how unwise it would be to move her into that cold room tonight. You are leaving tomorrow, and I wondered if you would let her have your room. How about it?"

Bill Andrews moved quickly. "Of course, Doctor," he said promptly. "Just give me a hand with these papers and books. I'll call a nurse to bring my clothes and shaving things. Let's go."

They moved off down the dim and quiet corridor to the door of the unlit sun room. Doctor Allen opened it, stepped inside and pressed the light switch.

"It's cold, Bill," he said almost apologetically. "Think you can stick it? I could arrange to send you home tonight if you'd rather."

"This is quite okay, Doc," Andrews told him. "I always sleep in a cold room at home. A grand view from that west window, dark as it is. I hope no one will come barging in here later?" he asked doubtfully noting the other bed. As he spoke the door opened and Alex Blair entered.

"You rang, Doctor?" she asked.

"Yes. See that 315 is in order and bring a couple of blankets to this room at once. Eunice Butler will be taking 315 directly. Appendectomy ruptured. I will be there immediately. Specials are on the way from Saint Luke's, but you are to remain with the patient until the first one arrives."

"Yes, Doctor," Alex answered.

"Don't you go off duty at eleven, Nurse?" Andrews asked. "You did when you were nursing me." He spoke aggrievedly. He had objected to her leaving him. The nurse nodded.

"Remain on duty until the special arrives, Blair," Allen told her quietly but firmly.

"Yes, Doctor," she answered evenly and slipped from the room.

Andrews grinned at the surgeon. "I wish I had your assurance, Doc," he jibed. "I wouldn't dare use that tone to my secretary or one of the girls at the plant. They'd quit before I could say 'Jack Robinson.' How come?"

"It's part of our training, Bill," Doctor Allen said. "Lives are at stake, and one can't afford to waste time on ceremony. Comfortable? More blankets will be along directly. Ask for anything you want or need, Bill. I'll see you in the morning."

" 'Night, Doc," the other called as the door closed.

Doctor Allen walked swiftly down the dimly lighted corridor to room 315 where Alex Blair was busy changing linen preparatory to the arrival of the patient from the operating room. The room was warm and almost luxurious, and the young man wondered if the Butlers would object to paying the price. Well, the girl could no doubt be moved a bit later on if another room became available. He opened the door and looked toward the elevator. Ann Mordock stood, small and belligerent, beside the desk in the alcove. Her blue eyes were dark with anger. She strode toward the young surgeon, every swift noiseless step showing her resentment.

"How dare you?" she demanded, her voice low but intense. "I won't have it. I simply will not have the schedule disarranged by you or anyone else."

The young man met her gaze with one quite as unflinching. "Just what do you propose to do about it?" he asked coldly.

"Nothing in this case, as you very well know. You have seen to that," she replied icily. "But I assure you it will never happen again."

She turned swiftly and went back to her desk fighting to keep the hot tears of humiliation from falling. She did not raise her head when the stretcher was wheeled past and the patient taken into 315. She knew it was unethical in the extreme—she should follow the stretcher—but somehow she didn't care. She remained at her desk until Eleanor Fields, the first special, arrived. Miss Fields paused at the desk and made the usual report as to her qualifications and her business, and was taken at once to 315 where Doctor Allen greeted her thankfully.

Miss Fields was tall and slender with dark eyes and blonde curly hair which she wore shoulder length and upon which her cap set becomingly, its black velvet band proclaiming her status in the profession. She smiled at the doctor and turned to thank Mordock.

"If I need anything I'll let you know, Nurse," she dismissed her.

Doctor Allen's eyes twinkled for a brief moment before he introduced Ann Mordock as the night supervisor of the west wing. The newcomer bit her lip, then smiled disarmingly.

"Sorry," she murmured as the supervisor moved toward the door. "We all look so much alike it is confusing sometimes, isn't it?"

Ann Mordock said nothing. She went out, the door closing softly behind her. But her blue eyes were dark with anger and hurt. She couldn't dispel the feeling that Douglas Allen was deliberately being disagreeable— getting even with her for refusing to fall down and worship him as the others did. Well, she would show him. She would report tonight's highhandedness to Miss Halliday. The superintendent was a stickler for rules and never took kindly to having the hospital schedules tampered with. Maybe Halliday could show that smarty-pants that he couldn't ride roughshod over people.

The patient in 315 had a bad night, and Doctor Allen was close by until things quieted down at four in the morning at which time he went over to the "Doctors' House" and flung himself on his bed to sleep for a couple of hours. At six he was up, showered, dressed, ate a hearty breakfast, and returned to the hospital next door. As he entered the front door, he once again knew that feeling of exaltation that he was here, associated with old Felix Mathews. It was nearly seven and already the place had begun to come alive. The superintendent, Miss Halliday, was just entering her office and called to him. He grinned to himself as he answered her summons.

"Another infringement of one of her precious rules, I suppose," he told himself ruefully. "Okay. *Mia culpa.*"

Miss Halliday greeted him coldly. Her expression was one of stern disapproval. "Sit down, Doctor Allen," she said, motioning to a chair across from her desk. "You have been with us now for a month or more?" It was a question, and the young man nodded.

"A month last Wednesday, Miss Halliday," he agreed.

"Then I'm sure you realize that the rules of this hospital are not at all unreasonable; that schedules are prepared carefully and are to be accepted and followed implicitly, unequivocally as the regular routine of the institution. No institution can work rhythmically without friction and with orderly precision unless there are rules and planned schedules. You should be aware of this?" Again it was a question.

"Right," Doctor Allen agreed, "except—"

"Without exception, Doctor Allen," the superintendent interrupted grimly.

"There we disagree," the young man said. "There are exceptions; there will always be exceptions. There are emergencies constantly occurring that can break the strictest rule and knock the most carefully prepared schedule into a cocked hat. Saving life is the important job of a hospital, Miss Halliday, not seeing that rules are kept and schedules followed to the letter. I suppose all this is because of my refusal to allow a patient of mine to be dumped into an icy sun room after an operation. I should be a pretty poor surgeon if I had allowed it, and I cannot understand a nurse's stubbornness in insisting upon it. Just what sort of a hospital is it that has no consideration or thought for its patients?"

Miss Halliday bridled. "You forget yourself, Doctor Allen," she said stiffly. "I'm sure—"

"I merely asked a rhetorical question, Miss Halliday,' the young man hastened to say. "I'm sure you and most of your staff will agree with me that the care of the patient, his welfare comes first, is of paramount importance. The rest is purely incidental."

The superintendent lost some of her belligerency as she gazed at the good looking young surgeon opposite.

"I am extremely sorry for this *contretemps*," she said less coldly. "I am sure the night supervisor of that wing was not fully aware of the circumstances. Mordock is one of our really splendid young women, and you will find her a fine and cooperative nurse. I am sure nothing of this nature will occur again, Doctor Allen."

"Thank you," the young man said as he moved toward the door. "I certainly hope it won't," he added to himself as he went on toward the elevator.

The patient in 315 was better this morning. Being young and strong, her reaction was swift. This was a lovely room, however, and the bed was out of this world. How wonderful to lie and doze for as long as she liked. The second special was already on duty and the patient's mother. The latter looked worried and Doctor Allen, after examining his patient, tried to quiet her fears. Through half-closed eyelids the girl in the hospital bed watched him. He could quite easily make one believe black was white and that somehow this hospital bill would be paid. She didn't intend worrying about it. What was the use? Doctor Allen would take care of everything. She dozed again while the surgeon talked to the girl's mother.

"Your daughter reacted splendidly, Mrs. Butler," he explained. "It was fortunate no time was lost."

"But the expense, Doctor," the woman whispered. "This room, these extra nurses."

"It was the only room available," the young man told her. "Perhaps in a day or two there will be a vacancy and she can be moved but just now—"

"It seems terrible to think of expense at this time, I know," the mother said chokingly, "but we are poor people."

"Don't let us worry about that, Mrs. Butler. First of all let us get our patient well. Do you know, my dear lady, that I have found things—problems, worries, fears—have a way of solving themselves. Your girl had a close call and we must pull together to see that she recovers. Forget everything but that."

The woman smiled with trembling lips. "You are very comforting and most optimistic, Doctor Allen," she said, wiping her eyes. "Given a little time I'm sure we can manage. We always have."

A breakfast tray arrived, and the nurse drew up a small table and urged the visitor to join her in a cup of coffee. But Mrs. Butler, after a long anxious look at her sleeping daughter, quietly withdrew. Doctor Allen followed.

"Have you breakfasted already, Mrs. Butler?" he asked.

"Oh, yes," the woman answered. "I have to get up at five most mornings. I do most of my housework before going down to the office. You see, I do bookkeeping and stenography at the Hill Laundry and my day begins early. Actually I am late this morning, but it is all right. Mr. Hill understands about Eunice. Thank you, Doctor Allen, for all you have done. You have been very kind. I have never liked hospitals, but this one is almost human."

The young surgeon smiled. "We should be," he replied. "We work with humans. There will be no need of special nurses after tomorrow. We were taking no chances you understand—one can't in cases such as this. But I'm sure everything will work out splendidly."

His eyes followed the woman as she walked down the corridor, and he shook his head. It was tough being poor especially when sickness and death struck. He knew Mlemorial's policy of never crowding its patients, of alowing almost unlimited time for the settlement of bills. The Chief boasted of never losing anything. Eventually bills were paid. Fortunately, Haddon Memorial was heavily endowed and so didn't suffer embarrassment by these delays. And somehow Douglas Allen was especially glad this cold winter morning that this was true. The Butlers were among the worthy poor—they needed time.

When he returned to the patient, he studied her chart and nodded with satisfaction. The nurse looked up as he returned it to the table from which he had taken it.

"Probably routine from now on," he told her, his gaze on the slight girl lying white and still on the narrow hospital bed.

"Successful operations usually are, aren't they?" the nurse agreed.

"Usually, but not always," the young man said.

"I know. The operation was successful but the patient died," the nurse quoted glibly.

Doctor Allen grinned at her and shook his head. "Let's not speak of such things," he chided. "Has she been conscious at all since you have been on duty?"

"Not entirely, Doctor. She opened her eyes once just after I came on and muttered something that sounded like 'Tell Joe' but that's all. She lapsed into unconsciousness or sleep. It was hard to tell which."

"She will probably sleep most of the day. I'll be in again later. When does your relief come? Three?"

"Right, Doctor," the girl answered.

"Thank you for helping us out, Miss—er—I don't believe I have ever heard your name."

"It's Mordock, Doctor. I have a cousin here, night supervisor in this wing. Have you met her, but of course you must have. She's a peach. Everyone is crazy about her. O-oh, I'm sorry, Doctor." She looked abashed.

Doctor Allen grinned, not too happily. "I've met your cousin, Miss Mordock," he said ruefully. "She is all you say she is but—" He turned as the door opened and Carey, the day supervisor entered. "Good morning!" he greeted her.

"Doctor Allen!" she said severely. "I have been waiting for you. When did you come in? Haven't you yet learned that a doctor is always accompanied by a nurse when making visits in this hospital? It is a rule we are careful to follow."

The young man's eyes sparkled for a moment then he grinned like a small boy caught in mischief. "I'm always forgetting about your endless rules and schedules, Miss Carey," he said ruefully. "Dear me, I'm afraid I shall never learn. Maybe it would be better if I quit my job here and moved over to Saint Luke's or maybe to General. Do you have lots of rules at Saint Luke's, Mordock?"

The supervisor swung about and examined the glowing girl who was smiling secretly.

"So you are Ann Mordock's cousin?" she said curiously. "Have you decided to join forces with us here at Memorial?"

Phyllis Mordock shook her head. "No. I like it at Saint Luke's. I only consented to come on as special because—oh, just because," she finished lamely. Her cheeks were flushed, and Doctor Allen thought she was very pretty. She was like her cousin but lacked her dignity and, he hoped, her stubbornness.

The supervisor turned to look at the patient. "Everything seems to be all right, doesn't it, Doctor?" she asked after a moment.

"The operation was a complete success," he replied.

They moved from the room and neither one saw a slim red tongue slip out between ruby lips as the nurse's impudent gaze followed them. The sound of a faint giggle from the patient in the bed startled her and she turned quickly.

"I saw you," chided the sick girl, "and I felt like doing it myself only I lacked the strength. Who's the dame? Fancies herself, doesn't she? Is she sweet on Doc Allen?" the voice was weak but the eyes were bright and mischievous.

"That, my dear patient, is her nibs the day supervisor. Carey's the name. Is she sweet on Doctor Allen? I wouldn't know that."

"Everyone's sweet on him," the sick girl said. "Even I am, believe it or not. Of course I haven't a chance, but that doesn't matter. A cat may look at a king, they tell us. He's simply swell. I wish I was a nurse."

"Why?" the nurse wanted to know. "And don't tell me it's so you could be near him and have a chance to know him better. You take it from me, my dear, doctors don't give a hoot for nurses. They work us to death, boss us around, and take all the credit when a patient recovers and give us the blame when one dies. I have no use for doctors, young, old or middle-aged. I wouldn't marry a doctor if he had a million dollars and offered every one of them to me, much as I like money. No, my dear, be thankful you don't have to associate with them. Have to 'Yes, Doctor. No, Doctor' them when you would like nothing better than to place the sole of your shoe on their anatomy where it would do the most good."

The girl in the bed was laughing and groaning as she held her side.

"Don't!" the nurse hissed sharply. "Stop it!" She put her hands on the girl's shoulders and held her still for a moment. "I ought to be shot," she whispered. "What sort of a nurse am I to go off the deep end over that breed? Please forgive me. Okay now? Want anything? Not that you could have anything if you did, but I just thought I would ask."

"Are you really and truly a nurse—a trained nurse?" the patient wanted to know.

"An R.N. do you mean? Sure. See that black band on my cap? That proves to the world at large that I have passed the state examinations and am qualified to demand nine dollars for every eight hours I'm in attendance upon a patient. I haven't collected many nine dollar fees yet, my dear," she said in a stage whisper. "I only passed my examination last week. And I mean to stick to private duty or special work. No general duty for me. Hospitals don't know how to appreciate their nurses—some of their nurses," she qualified. "Take my cousin, Ann Mordock, for instance. She's night supervisor here in this wing. You'll love her. She works herself to a frazzle trying to follow the crazy schedules and tough rules Halliday, the superintendent here, maps out. I'd go nuts. But Ann loves it even though she's getting thinner by the minute. I'm trying to get her to quit and go into private duty, too, but she adores old Doc Mathews, Chief of Staff here. Oh, he's almost in his dotage and he's smart as all get-out, but I tell her she might better pin her hopes on a younger man—there are plenty only too willing."

She stopped suddenly. The eyes of the patients were drooping. Well, she had talked her to sleep. But the girl in the bed murmured drowsily:

"Go on talking, nurse. You're cute. I like to listen to you."

"You shut your eyes and sleep, my dear. That's what you need. I'll be here until three this afternoon and maybe I'll get another glimpse of your dreamboat. 'Rock-a-bye, baby, on the tree top,' " she sang softly and smiling contentedly, the patient slept.

CHAPTER THREE

ANN MORDOCK was, perhaps, Alex Blair's closest friend among the girls in Haddon Memorial. They were alike in that each took her job seriously and planned a future devoted to nursing. They saw but little of each other, and it was only when Alex was assigned to night duty in the west wing that they worked together. But from Alex's advent as a student nurse, she had liked and admired the older girl. Somehow she had a feeling that Ann could be trusted, and the feeling was quite mutual. They had occasionally gone to the movies, to church, and for long walks together and Alex had discovered a kinship with the quiet night supervisor.

When Douglas Allen arrived, there was quite a stir among the younger nurses, and even the older ones seemed to move with quicker step and work with brighter eye and readier smile. Only these two—Ann Mordock and Alex Blair—failed to join the crop of admirers of the young assistant surgeon. Both girls were quick to acknowledge the young man's ability but were cool and even aloof in his presence. Ann had quietly but definitely refused his invitations to dine and dance, while Alex had managed to keep him from even voicing such invitations. Needless to say, the young man felt their unfriendliness and resented it.

However, he had no thought of revenge after his *contretemps*, as the superintendent called it, with Ann Mordock. In fact, he had quite promptly forgotten it. He did wonder, though, what had become of her when he had occasion at night to visit the west wing and saw no trace of her. One of the older nurses was on duty as night supervisor and, being a stanch admirer of the young man, was only too eager to cooperate with his every wish. Nothing was said concerning the change and if he sensed an added coldness in Alex Blair's manner toward him he pretended complete indifference.

And it wasn't until one evening a week or so later when he and Ellen Ridley, the night superintendent and Doctor Mathew's granddaughter, were dining at Castle Grill, that he discovered what had happened to Ann Mordock. They had been discussing the continued nurse shortage, and Ellen spoke of Mordock's leave of absence or whatever it was.

"I never approved of Halliday giving the job of supervisor to Mordock in the first place," Ellen Ridley said as her gaze swept the crowded room in search of a familiar face. "What if she did take special training, she's far too young and mild for it, Doug. I wonder why she quit, for I have an idea that's what it amounts to. Halliday won't tell. I bet the old girl put the screws on her for some infringement of her precious rules. Yet that seems sort of odd, too, because Mordock has always been a special pet of hers—she and Alex Blair. Those two are almost inhumanly perfect, painfully so. Don't you agree? I bet even you have never made time with either of them," she jibed.

"Right the first time, Ellen," the young man answered ruefully. "Swell nurses, though."

"Just the same I'm surprised that Halliday would consent to let her go out of the hospital just because old lady Brixton demanded it. Of course I know the Brixtons have been generous to Memorial in the past, and Grandfather sets considerable store by them, still nurses at Memorial are scarce and we need every one we have."

"Is that where Mordock is, Ellen?" Doctor Allen asked. "Don't tell me she has lost her job here because—"

"Because what?" the other asked curiously.

"Nothing. I just wondered. But I intend finding out."

"Now you're being aggravating, Doctor," the young woman told him, examining him with interest. "Don't tell me you have been turned down cold by one of the ice princesses, Doug."

"Don't be ridiculous," Doctor Allen retorted curtly. "Eat your dinner. I have to be back at the hospital in half an hour."

"No wonder Grandfather sets such store by you, Doctor," the night superintendent jibed. "Don't you ever relax and forget your duty as an up and coming surgeon? *I* never intend letting my job monopolize my entire life. One has only one life to live, and I propose getting the most out of it. I guarantee I'll be a better nurse for it—a more sympathetic and understanding one, anyway. Don't glare at me like that. I'm nearly through and, believe it or not, I, am due at the hospital in a few minutes. Or had you forgotten? So, you see, you haven't a monopoly on duty and ethical practice. Come on, pal, let's go."

Haddon Memorial was ablaze with light from roof to basement and as Douglas Allen's green coupe slid into the parking space near the entrance to receiving, the young surgeon knew a surge of pride as he always did upon approaching the huge conglomerate building. It had been a hard climb, but at last he glimpsed his goal. As he strode across the snowy gravel, the young woman with him laid a restraining hand on his arm.

"Remember me, Doctor? You're supposed to be my escort this evening. Have pity on my feet if not on my feelings."

"I'm sorry," he murmured, slowing his pace. "Why do you wear such heels? You'll ruin your feet."

"Mmm," she murmured, moving close to his side as they neared the illumined receiving room. "It isn't the heel's it's the pace you set that causes me pain, my dear Douglas. And when on duty my shoes are as strictly utilitarian as your own, but I dressed up for my date with you—just in case you haven't noticed."

Doctor Allen stood still and held the young woman at arms length while he gazed at her admiringly. She was tall, slender, blonde, and almost beautiful. She was wearing a black fur coat and small fur hat that were most becoming. She carried herself with pride, at time arrogance—and while most people admired her there were many who resented that arrogant manner. At the hospital she was tolerated because of her relationship to the Chief of Staff who was adored by everyone. But Marie Halliday, the superintendent, and most of the nurses felt she took advantage of that relationship to ignore rules and alter schedules to suit her whims. One and all felt they would be glad if she took her undisputed charms, though none too pleasing personality, to some other hospital.

There were rumors she might become a fixture here if and when she married Douglas Allen, her grandfather's assistant, but while he was seen with her more often than with any other girl, doubts were expressed if he was in love with her. The staff as a whole considered his attentions those of expediency rather than amorousness.

And the young man himself had moments when he wished Ellen Ridley were different—less aggressively professional, more sympathetic and womanly. Somehow Ellen harbored the conviction that she was essential to the efficient running of Haddon Memorial; that without her all-pervading influence the hospital would cease to function effectively. He had jeered good-naturedly at her air of authority, had reminded her that Haddon had operated successfully long before she was born—but to no

25

avail. She assured him that her grandfather was far too gullible and too easy-going, and that she was there to keep him from coming a cropper. No, Douglas Allen doubted if he would care to marry a nurse, and yet one or two nurses he could name were most attractive though cool and aloof. These thoughts flashed through his mind as he stood face to face with Ellen Ridley. His hands dropped, and he opened the door and followed her inside.

The room was empty except for a nurse busy cleaning up after an emergency. Ellen Ridley's high heels clicked on the polished floor as she passed quickly through the room to the hall and stairs beyond. The nurse looked up from her work and smiled faintly, but the night superintendent failed to acknowledge the implied greeting. The young surgeon, however, paused.

"Had a busy evening, Marsh? These hills combined with this vile weather certainly add to our labors up here, don't they? What was it this time? Car accident?"

"Hit and run driver, apparently. The man was badly hurt. Doctor Mathews is operating now."

"The deuce you say!" he exclaimed and hurried from the room, taking the stairs two at a time. He shed overcoat and hat as he ran, and reached the elevator just as it stopped to disgorge its load of evening visitors. He pressed the button for the operating room, and was in time to see the stretcher being rolled out. Divested of gloves and operating room regalia, the Chief was scrubbing when he reached the washroom, and turned as his assistant entered.

"A nasty job, Doug. A very nasty job." He sighed and dried his wet hands on the towel held out to him. "We did the best we could but it will be nip and tuck if he survives. Shock as much as anything although he lost a great deal of blood. I wish you had been here, boy."

"I wish I had, Chief," the younger man said. "We weren't gone long. Ellen and I went over to the Castle Grill for dinner. It couldn't have been much over an hour. I'll run down and look at him if you like, although—"

"Do that, son," The man sounded weary, and Doctor Allen felt a sense of guilt at being absent from the hospital for even an hour. The Chief was getting too old for night work.

Alex Blair stood beside the bed of an apparently dying

man, her fingers on his wavering pulse, when Douglas Allen entered. He joined her and took the thin wrist from her. He gave brief, decisive orders. A transfusion was indicated, prepare saline solution for intravenous injections, oxygen, all the paraphernalia for a fight, and Alex moved quickly and efficiently. The two worked steadily throughout the long night. Once the young surgeon glanced at the nurse beside him.

"Past midnight, Nurse," he pointed out. "You could be relieved, you know."

The girl shook her head. "I'll stay," she said simply.

The one o'clock lunch came and neither noticed. It was five when the first signs of returning vitality began to show in the faint trace of color in lips and cheeks and the steadier pulse. Doctor Allen straightened.

"He'll do now." He smiled and received an answering smile from Alex. It was somewhat wavering, but was the first notice she had ever taken of him, and the young man experienced an unexpected lift of spirit. "Run along. The floor nurse can carry on until the seven o'clock relief arrives. I'll stick around for a few minutes just to be sure." He placed a paternal hand on the girl's shoulder. "Together we've done a good night's work, Blair. The Chief didn't hold out much hope for him. And by the way, who is he?"

Alex shook her head. "There were no identification marks about him. His clothes were shabby and, while he wasn't exactly unkempt, he looked like a poor man. The Chief doesn't think he comes from these parts, and yet no luggage of any sort was found near where he was picked up. No doubt the police will know soon." It was a long speech, and Doctor Allen noted the concern in the tired face of the young nurse.

"Of course," he answered. "The police will identify him." The door opened and Doctor Hammond, the resident, entered.

"Beat it, you two," he told them quietly. "I'll take over from this point on. Good morning to you both!"

For once his puckish grin was absent, and Alex left quickly. The hospital was silent. Not yet were there signs of awakening. The girl went swiftly along the dimly lighted corridors and through the short enclosed walk to the nurses' section. The morning was bitterly cold. She was hungry, too, and hoped to find food in the kitchen. She opened the door and went in, and was surprised and relieved to find Mrs. Martin bustling about already.

"You sit right down in that rocker, my dear," the woman told her, drawing it closer to the gas oven. "I know all about it. Doctor Allen called me just a minute ago. Fortunately I was getting up anyway—bread to make for the hospital, and I like to get an early start. Don't move, Alex. I'll have your breakfast in a jiffy."

And that is exactly what she did. Orange juice, oatmeal with cream, buttered toast with poached egg in milk, hot coffee and fresh molasses cookies. She ate heartily and with enjoyment while the housemother watched in satisfaction. Alex Blair was a special favorite of hers, and it pleased her to do little kindnesses for the girl.

Now the young nurse laughed as she drained her cup. "I feel well repaid for working overtime, Mrs. Martin," she said, leaning back in her chair. "Food never tasted so good. I didn't realize how hungry I was. And come to think of it, we didn't touch our midnight lunch—too concerned and busy."

Mrs. Martin shook her head. "Nurses aren't often like you are, Alex," she said regretfully. "But be careful you don't carry your devotion to duty too far. Of course you are young and strong now, but there is such a thing as crowding the mourners, as the saying is. It's the willing ones who have work piled on them. Don't let them do it, my dear. Confine yourself to the schedule—the ten hours Miss Halliday sets such store by. That one is a stickler for schedules, but I'm willing to wager my new winter bonnet she won't penalize you for working sixteen hours and without food. Not Marie Halliday."

Alex rose to her feet. She stretched her arms high above her head in healthy relaxation. "Don't worry about me, Mrs. Martin," she said, yawning. "It was worth it to see the return of color to that poor man's face and his heart get back its steady beat. Nursing can be very rewarding, you know."

"I wish more of the girls thought so," the housemother murmured. "Now run along to bed and try to sleep until mid-afternoon if you can. I intend fixing your lunch right here in my kitchen, so don't feel you have to go over to the dining room for it. Good night, my dear. Sleep well!"

And Alex left the room with a light step in spite of her weariness. She was glad it happened to be her day off. She had planned to telephone Ann and go over to the park for some skating, but just now the thought of bed was too tempting. The skating could wait for another day. She yawned and stretched again in tired relaxation as she prepared for bed. She was glad the housemother liked her. It was wonderful to be appreciated. It was thoughtful, too, of Doctor Allen to telephone Mrs. Martin and see that she had a hot breakfast, but he need not have bothered. Her thoughts flew to Ann Mordock. He had been hateful to her. She hoped Ann would come back to the hospital. She missed her. She wished she had stayed on. She had a premonition that the superintendent was considering offering her a supervisor's job. She didn't want it. She liked general duty nursing. She knew that Ellen Ridley was not too friendly with either her or Ann, and wondered why. There had been a great deal of gossip around the hospital that the night superintendent was in love with Doctor Allen. Her lip curled. She was welcome to him if she could get him. He was far too conceited for her taste. Even if he had been especially kind this past night it didn't mean anything, and altered not a whit her feeling regarding him. She wanted nothing to do with him. Let Ridley have him if she wanted him and could get him. A little smile touched her lips and was still there when she fell asleep.

CHAPTER FOUR

A FEW DAYS later Alex was summoned to the superintendent's office and informed that her efficiency and unwavering devotion to duty had been noted and were about to be rewarded. She was to become acting night supervisor in the west wing—the position left vacant by Ann Mordock's leave of absence. Alex stiffened there before the superintendent and rebellion stirred in her heart.

"Thank you, Miss Halliday," she said quietly, "for your kindness and commendation, but I do not want to be

29

a supervisor. I like general duty nursing and much prefer remaining in my present position. I am sure there are others much better fitted for the position than I."

"And I am sure you will reconsider your decison, Blair," Miss Halliday said coldly, disapprovingly. She did not like the idea of anyone questioning her judgment. "The west wing is sadly in need of a night supervisor. Mordock disappointed us by demanding a leave of absence. When she returns, if she returns, the position will no longer be hers. You must see that it is a promotion, my dear girl, a reward for excellent service rendered the hospital. We in the nursing profession are pledged to serve wherever the need arises. None of us expect to lead easy lives, Blair," she went on. "The very fact of our entering the nursing profession proves that, or should. We have to make sacrifices, suffer discomforts, rebuffs, criticisms and hardships but a good nurse never welshes. Doctor Mathews and I have talked the matter over and have decided that you should be given your chance at the opening in the west wing. We felt sure you would appreciate the honor and the trust we have in you. Think it over and let me know as soon as possible—this evening at latest. We are most anxious to have the matter settled. That is all, Blair, and thank you for being helpful and cooperative. Good afternoon."

Alex left the office with a feeling of complete frustration. She knew she would take the job much as she disliked the idea. Helpful? Cooperative? That's what came of being a good nurse—of working hard and attending strictly to the business at hand. She wished she could talk to someone—to Ann Mordock. Maybe she could get in touch with her.

Ann answered the telephone when Alex called her, and suggested having tea at the Madison Tea Room at four that afternoon. And Alex left the hospital to walk the long snowy mile to the meeting place, wondering what Ann's advice would be. She recalled the older girl's satisfaction in her position and the quiet, pleasant manner she had toward the nurses under her. Would she advise her to accept the job, or did she still have a notion that she would come back to the hospital and take up where she had left off. Alex didn't know.

The girls met in the small lobby of the popular tea room and sat for a moment enjoying the quaint atmosphere of the place. Alex thought Ann looked far from happy, and wished she dared ask the cause. On the other hand, Ann thought she had never seen her friend more lovely and frankly told her so.

"Are things going well at the hospital, Alex?" she asked as they found a table in the big sunny room beyond. "Do you know, I miss it. In a way this is much easier, of course, and there is little or no night work, but just the same I liked the bustle and change at Haddon." She sighed deeply. "Oh, the Brixtons are wonderful to me—not at all demanding or inconsiderate, but I don't know, I guess I'm just a hospital nurse. Private duty is far too monotonous to suit me."

"Much more money though," reminded Alex.

"Oh, money!" the other scoffed. "If it had been money I was after I should have chosen a different profession—the law, stage or even business. But I chose to become a nurse."

"Did you really like being a supervisor, Ann?" Alex asked as she nibbled a piece of crisp toast.

"At first I didn't," Ann confessed. "But after a while I really liked it. That extra authority was sweet to my ego, I suppose. And I felt sure I was a good supervisor until—" She paused and bit her lip. "Perhaps I was too severe, too determined to hold to the strict schedule Miss Halliday had prepared that once room plans were drawn up no changes could be made. Every room in the west wing was occupied. Only the sun room was vacant, and only recently at that. Doctor Allen knew that—knew it as well as I did. Why didn't he try to find a vacant room in one of the other wings, over in the east wing perhaps. They seem never to be crowded over there. But no, he had to pick on me. Had to show his authority and undermine mine. Oh, well, I hope he is satisfied. I'm sorry, Alex," she murmured contritely. "I shouldn't have wailed on your shoulder like this. What's on your mind, darling?"

"Miss Halliday wants me to take your old job, Ann, and I don't want it. I'm a general duty nurse and I want to remain so. I like it. I don't want the responsibility of being a supervisor, and I feel sure some of the other nurses would resent my having it. I told Miss Halliday as much, and she simply ignored my excuses—talked about the duty of a nurse to accept responsibility when offered, never to welsh at difficulties or, in other words, refuse to take any job the management might feel like dumping into her lap. I feel as if I had been run over by a steam roller. What am I to do?"

"Do? Why, just what I did when she railroaded me into taking the job, Alex. Of course I had that extra training behind me, but just the same I didn't want to be a supervisor or thought I didn't. But I took it just as you will, and try to get what pleasure you can out of it and here's hoping Doctor Allen won't spring any of his tricks on you as he did on me. And, by the way, what would you do if he did?"

"Probably just what you did," Alex replied. "But I don't want the job, Ann. I wish I could think of a good convincing excuse that would make her decide against me."

Ann Mordock laughed and patted the hand of her friend. "Don't take it so hard, Alex. Really it isn't so bad. Night supervisors have it much easier in the west wing than in some of the others. Until lately it was never full to capacity. But even if it is, the nurses who work in that wing are much easier to handle than some of the others. Most of them are older and seem to take their work seriously. I don't know why the youngsters avoid that wing unless that's another of the superintendent's ideas. Could be, you know."

Alex nodded. "I don't know how I ever happened to work there so much," she murmured. "I have often wondered about that, but I like it over there."

"It's sort of restricted territory, you know. It's the old part and people hereabouts, the better families like the rooms, and after all they are the ones who can afford to pay the price. That's why the older nurses work there, too. The patients demand nurses they have had before". She laughed at Alex's puzzled expression. "Oh, I'm not intimating that you are old, my dear, or that I am either—it's just that you and I are quiet and take our work seriously. Some one or two or three must have mentioned the fact of our efficiency, or we should not have been stationed there. I don't know if you will consider that as a compliment or an insult, Alex. I sort of liked the idea myself."

Alex said nothing for a moment, then she raised troubled eyes to her friend's face. "Then you advise me to take the job, Ann? You don't mind them giving it to me?"

"Don't be silly. Why should I mind? And as for my advice about accepting the position—I doubt if you will have any choice, my dear. As I said before when they gave the job to me, I was simply railroaded into it. That's Halliday's system. That lady gets what she wants by direct methods. In her case it works."

The girls separated at the door and each went her separate way. Alex reached the hospital, and felt none of the pleasure she usually experienced as she circled the huge pile of masonry that bore the name of Haddon Memorial Hospital. She mounted the stairs to her room and stood for a moment gazing out at the wintry landscape.

Down in the superintendent's office, Miss Halliday sat at her desk. Complaints had reached her from the east wing of insubordination, impudence, malingering and broken rules. And yet she felt the rules were by no means harsh—no harsher than in other first class hospitals. She wished it were possible to hire only middle-aged nurses, or at least those past their impulsive and romantic first youth. These fresh young chits in the perky caps they always wore at provocative tilts, never as they were supposed to be worn straight on their heads, were not easy to manage. She wondered about their training schools. She wished more of her own specially trained girls would remain with her, but always there were several of each class who married almost at once upon graduation and the rest invariably went into private work, where, of course, the pay was better. She wondered what the world was coming to—what the nursing profession was heading toward. It was growing increasingly difficult to maintain the high standard for which Haddon Memorial had for generations been noted.

Even the student nurses seemed to lack something of the awareness of the duties of a nurse, failed to understand or were unable to realize that wearing a becoming cap and uniform was not the whole of nursing, that being

33

a trained nurse required hard work, selflessness, the determination to devote their time and energy, their heart and soul to the aiding in the care of the sick and helpless. Over in the newer wings, where the student nurses received most of their practical training there was always more or less friction. The superintendent supposed that association with the younger nurses was, perhaps, not the best of examples for these youngsters, but there seemed no way out. Because of the nurse shortage hospitals had to endure a great deal. Too much criticism or the curtailing of privileges, meant simply that the nurse in question would walk out. She sighed deeply. If only there were more nurses—more girls like Alex Blair and, yes, Ann Mordock whom she hoped would return to them before too long. She hoped Alex would accept the position offered her even if only temporarily. Of course she would, Miss Halliday had little doubt of that, but she hoped it would be accepted wholeheartedly and without reservations.

Upon her graduation Doctor Mathews had urged Alex Blair to become a surgical nurse—his own surgical nurse. They had worked well together, and while the girl had served her required time in surgery, she had wanted straight nursing—all kinds of nursing. Alex had glowed with enthusiasm as she talked with them and they had felt some of her youthful ardor, and each had experienced an upsurge of professional zeal because of it. Now the superintendent wondered if this move of hers would cause talk— jealousy, adverse criticism or unpleasant discussions among the staff. Well, she would have to endure it as she had other unpleasantnesses.

And as she went down to dinner that evening, Alex stopped at the superintendent's office and announced her decision to accept the position offered. She told herself there was no surprise in the older woman's face as she smiled and held out her hand.

"I had an idea you wouldn't let me down, Blair," she told her warmly. "I felt I could count on you in this crisis. Thank you, my dear. I feel sure you will never regret it."

"I certainly hope I won't," Alex told herself as she walked on down the stairs to the dining room in the basement. And it was while they were at dinner that the superintendent announced that Alex Blair was to become night supervisor in the west wing beginning tonight. She asked for her the cooperation and consideration that was her due. It was a hard position for the girl who, sensitive as she was to the suppressed antagonism of some of her fellow nurses, wished the announcement could have been made less publicly. Suddenly, Bradley, perhaps the oldest nurse in the hospital, began to clap softly and after a moment others joined, and Alex rose to her feet to thank them. Her eyes were very bright and her voice was husky as she hoped she would make a satisfactory supervisor, at least she would do her best, with their help. Miss Halliday smiled and left the room—a suddenly silent room—and Alex felt she must get away for a moment alone. She pushed back her chair and quickly followed the superintendent, and felt rather than heard the sudden resumption of conversation with the closing of the door. What was said Alex had no way of knowing.

She went directly to her room, there to try to calm her troubled thoughts and to gain courage to tackle the new job. She would do the best she could and somehow she was confident of success even if she had no special training and didn't want to be a supervisor. Evidently the Chief and superintendent felt her capable of the work, or they wouldn't have suggested it. One or two supervisors in other parts of the hospital had taken advanced training, and even Ann Mordock had gone to Columbia for three months intensive preparation. Just why had they given her this post without that training? She didn't know and experienced no thrill of attainment. In fact she felt weak and almost afraid.

She squared her shoulders and her bright head went up. She was a nurse, wasn't she, and as such must be willing to meet what emergencies came with courage and confidence. But just the same she wondered what Ellen Ridley would say. She didn't happen to be at dinner tonight. She had criticized Miss Halliday's judgment in giving a supervisor's job to Ann Mordock, and Ann was four years older. No doubt she would object even more to her replacing Ann. She wondered just why Ridley disliked her—disliked Ann, also, or at least she wasn't at all friendly to them. She sighed, adjusted her cap so that it was perfectly straight on her bright head and left the room to take up her new duties in the west wing.

And down in the superintendent's office Ellen Ridley and Douglas Allen were talking with Miss Halliday. The Chief's granddaughter was emphatic in her criticism of the promotion of Alex Blair to the position of night supervisor in the important west wing. Not only was Alex untrained but she was far too young for the responsibility and with the shortage of nurses she felt the hospital could ill afford to lose her. Everyone knew that supervisors did little except see that everything ran smoothly; they did no actual nursing.

"I agree with Grandfather, Miss Halliday," Ellen Ridley stated firmly. "Blair should have stuck to surgery. She was an excellent surgical nurse, and Haddon needed her. I cannot understand Grandfather agreeing to this change."

"Doctor Mathews and I have discussed it thoroughly, Miss Ridley," the superintendent answered coolly.

Doctor Allen was frank in his disapproval of the change. The west wing needed a woman of experience, one not easily maneuvered by either nurse or patient.

"Or doctor either," Miss Halliday reminded him somewhat acidly and knew a feeling of satisfaction as the young man appeared chagrined. However, he recovered quickly and continued his objections.

"You realize the west wing is made up of special and high priced rooms to which some of the town's prominent citizens come by preference because they are familiar with them?"

"Certainly," the superintendent agreed, "and that is why most of the nurses there are well known, experienced women. There is little or no danger of flirtatious males losing their heads over their pretty nurses in the west wing, Doctor," she went on coldly.

"How about losing their heads over a pretty young supervisor?" he asked.

"No danger of Blair countenancing anything of the sort," Miss Halliday said firmly. "She isn't the type."

Doctor Allen snorted and assured her that most men, and women, too, wanted to be nursed by good looking young nurses. "The older the patient, the keener his desire for youth and beauty to serve him," he contended a bit facetiously. "Helps the old morale."

The superintendent sniffed in disdain. "The more fools

they," she retorted. "It's efficiency we pride ourselves on and it's what patients pay for, Doctor Allen. People don't come here to be amused or entertained; they come to us to be healed of their illnesses. The sooner people forget the romance of nursing and realize its practical uses, the better for everyone—nurses included."

Ellen Ridley jeered at the contention that plain and elderly nurses were to be preferred to the pretty ones. Douglas Allen applauded her. And the superintendent bit her lip and glared from one to the other.

"All this is beside the point," she said coldly. "Blair is a fine, capable nurse. The fact that she is in her early twenties has nothing to do with it." Miss Halliday didn't take kindly to criticism. "Blair has a level head, and will probably get more actual work out of the nurses under her than anyone I know, because, you see, she herself is not afraid of work. The fact that she is young is in this instance to her advantage because she will be able to stand the arduous routine better than an older woman could." She sighed in exasperation. "Somehow the young nurses today, the average young nurses, seem to find the demands here at Haddon too much for them. I, myself, cannot understand it."

"I can, Miss Halliday," Ellen Ridley retorted, although she knew she was treading on dangerous ground. "It's the rules, the formidable rules and regulations, the schedules you and the Chief set such store by. They are altogether too unreasonable. Time and time again I have tried to convince Grandfather of that fact, but he's too stubborn to see my point. He likes rules and regulations. I don't much. It's a wonder to me the nurses you have here continue to endure them as well as they do. I know, if I were expected to abide by them, I should be inclined to either give them a wide berth or change to some other and less restricted hospital. Young people nowadays have to have freedom to work out their own ideas. They won't be fenced in as their mothers and grandmothers were. I know you don't like my saying this, but it is the way I feel, and you probably know by this time that I say what I mean without mincing words."

For a moment the young surgeon experienced a feeling of pity for the superintendent who was having difficulty in controlling herself. Doctor Allen knew this tall young nurse would never have dared speak as she was doing if she were anyone but the Chief's granddaughter. He thought that she was taking an unfair advantage of the older woman. He felt, too, that he would thoroughly enjoy spanking the pert female beside him, and for a moment he heartily disliked her.

The superintendent's face had been a study in conflicting expressions during Ellen Ridley's tirade which was uttered for the most part in the young woman's smooth, confident even slightly arrogant voice. She said nothing for a moment, reminding herself that she must not lose her temper—must not forget that Ellen Ridley was the Chief's adored granddaughter, and not to be snubbed and put in her place. Oh well, she might be leaving soon. Doctor Mathews had spoken of a young man in Chicago to whom his granddaughter was tentatively engaged. He had stressed the adjective somewhat ruefully. So Miss Halliday merely spoke coolly and not too severely.

"Doctor Mathews and I have gone over these rules very carefully, Miss Ridley," she said evenly. "And you will please notice that a great many of our nurses have been with us a long time, some have actually grown old in the service. And you will notice, too, that it is seldom necessary to discipline one of our Haddon trained nurses because of infringement of one of the rules you object to so much. After all, Miss Ridley, she went on, "Pardon? I didn't hear you," as the young woman murmured something under her breath. "Please repeat that remark," she added stiffly.

"I merely mentioned the fact that what you don't know need cause you no sleeplessness, Miss Halliday," she explained almost defiantly.

"And that means?"

"You don't for one moment think that your precious rules are obeyed to the letter by the girls in the new part, do you?"

The superintendent straightened in her chair. "I have confidence in both my day and night supervisors, Miss Ridley," she said coldly.

"Tattletale!" hissed Douglas Allen, and the young woman had the grace to blush.

"I'm sorry," she said. And Miss Halliday went on as if the little byplay had gone unnoticed.

"After all, Miss Ridley," she said quietly, although

her usually rather pale face was warm with color, "this is a hospital. People come here in the hope of procuring relief, help, and the return to health. I have no patience with laxity in the nursing profession. I can make no excuse for the letting down of the rather rigid bars—the condoning of laziness or indifference in those caring for the sick. Our girls are trained to give their patients every consideration and care. Here, because of the shortage of nurses, the eight hour working schedule cannot always be maintained. Sometimes a longer working day is obligatory but we try to make things as pleasant and considerate as possible, in spite of the rigid rules. But I have been in hospitals—you have, too, no doubt—where it is next to impossible to get a nurse to answer promptly and pleasantly a patient's request for the mere simple everyday requirements. There is none of that here, I am happy and proud to say. Our nurses take bedside nursing seriously. I have yet to receive a complaint from one of our patients of neglect on that score. I hope if it is ever necessary for you to need the benefit of nursing care that you will be as well and efficiently served." She rose to her feet, a tall, handsome woman in her middle fifties, and smiled almost maternally on the equally tall, slim young woman across the desk.

Ellen Ridley's laugh was light, somewhat derisive. "Don't worry about me, Miss Halliday," she answered, moving to the door. "Live and let live has always been my motto, and I won't expect too much from my nurse if I ever require one. You should remember that these days there are aides and practical nurses for that bedside nursing you boast of." She was smiling as she left the room, and Miss Halliday shook her head sadly. What was her beloved profession coming to? She turned in her seat and raised her eyes to the picture of Florence Nightingale on the wall behind her chair and to the pledge of service hanging beside it. How dared anyone take that pledge lightly? Forgetting the presence of the young surgeon, she repeated it aloud almost solemnly. It was beautiful—it was like taking vows.

" 'I solemnly pledge myself before God, and in the presence of this company, to pass my life in purity and to practice my profession faithfully. I will abstain from whatever is deleterious and mischievous and will not take or knowingly administer any harmful drug. I will

39

do all in my power to elevate the standard of my profession and will hold in confidence all personal matters committed to my keeping and all family affairs coming to my knowledge in the practice of my calling. With loyalty will I endeavor to aid the physician in his work and devote myself to the welfare of those committed to my care.' "

"Don't take Ridley too seriously, Miss Halliday," Douglas Allen said quietly. "She has been badly spoiled. She will learn. How she will learn! Life has a way of slapping us down, you know. He whistled softly as he left the room.

"Well," Miss Halliday told herself as she turned again to the pile of case histories on her desk, "the nurses in this hospital are living up to that pledge, or I shall know the reason why."

It was some time later that she realized that all this wordy discussion was due to the fact that Ellen Ridley objected to Alex Blair being given the position of night supervisor in the west wing. Just why should she object? It was really none of her business. A frown of perplexity marred for a moment the smooth brow of the superintendent and she stared unseeing at the work before her. Then her face cleared. Doctor Allen understood, and she felt sure he didn't approve of the Chief's granddaughter—which was, she felt just as sure, an excellent state of affairs. Perhaps there was some connection there with the main issue. Time would tell.

CHAPTER FIVE

THE BIG WHITE clock on the wall warned for the half hour, the sound low and musical. And Miss Halliday shoved aside the pile of work on her polished desk and prepared to leave the room. Once again her eyes sought the picture of Florence Nightingale and the pledge of service hanging beside it; then her shoulders straightened and her white head lifted proudly. She must be on her way. It was time for morning inspection—time to join the Chief and Doctor Tom Hammond in their daily tour of the hospital. To the superintendent this slow walk along the corridors, into private rooms, and through the wards was a pilgrimage of love. She was considered an austere woman, one with little or no sympathy, and it was true that she had none with shirkers or malingerers. Only those in need of advice whether mental, moral, or physical, knew the rich depths of the great soul of Marie Halliday.

This morning she followed the Chief of Staff without her usual buoyancy of spirit. She had not slept well. Ellen Ridley's glib criticism rankled. And perhaps it was partly due to the weather. Bleak and sunless, a riotous winter wind buffeted the tall cedars surrounding the hospital, dashed icy particles of snow against windows and brought shivers to sensitive patients. The Chief's expression was unnaturally grave. Only Doctor Hammond, the jovial resident, was his usual puckish self. He winked at Miss Abigail Milton, known throughout the hospital as "Old Sourpuss" and was surprised to see her blush, so he winked again and made a wry face behind the Chief's broad back. Out of his capacious pocket he brought forth a candy bar which he made a great show of slipping to her without the others seeing. A piggy bank went to decorate the smoothly drawn spread of one of the city's bankers—a prim bachelor fond of pointing out the need of saving the pennies. The banker sniffed disdainfully, but fingered it almost caressingly. There was a fuzzy kitten for rich old lady Nettleworth, who was reputed to be worth millions, and who suffered from spells of the most abject misery fearing her selfish and neglectful relatives wished only for her death. A book of children's verse fell into the hands of young Sally Blain, dreaming that some day she might become a child's governess, although everyone in the hospital knew she would never walk again. A few gum drops were the portion for old Grandpa White who kept his false teeth in a glass beside his bed but never wore them. On and on moved the small procession, and still forthcoming from Hammond's wife and bottomless pocket came the small gifts for those hopelessly ill, for those appointed to die, and for those who just now found life unbearable.

Miss Halliday often wondered where the resident got hold of his odd assortment of gifts, and how he seemed to know what would bring a smile to thin lips or a gleam of amusement or interest to bleak eyes. If the Chief saw what went on he gave no sign, but somehow the day seemed to grow brighter with the passing of the trio, and when at last they reached the children's ward on the top floor, all three were smiling and were greeted by the youngsters with shouts of welcome.

Old Sam Fletcher looked up from his book as the young night supervisor entered his room. There had been a time when he had resented the making a supervisor of his favorite nurse, fearing she would have less time to devote to him. But he found that each night Alex made it a point to visit each patient in the west wing often to see that everything was satisfactory and inquire if anything might be needed for added comfort.

"How you making out, Nurse?" he now wanted to know. "I've had my TPR recorded, the usual dose of some vile concoction given, and you have nothing to do. I'll wager it seems queer for you to have all that done for you, doesn't it?"

"Oh, I still have my share of that sort of thing, Mr. Fletcher," Alex told him. "I don't mind and I guess I'm doing all right. I'm not so scared now."

The old man smiled. "Do you know that I fought against your taking the job, my dear?" he asked. "Being a selfish old codger, I was afraid I'd never see you, but I have an idea I was crying before I was hurt. If it's a promotion I'm glad you've got it, only don't let them put anything over on you. You'll be a success of course," he went on. "You needn't have been scared. It's the cocky ones who come a cropper every time. Like stage fright, it's the normal state of mind for one to be scared when making a first appearance you know."

"Well, I was being perfectly normal, then," the girl replied, as she gave a swift, professional glance about the room. "And no reading after lights out, Mr. Fletcher," she warned. "Nine o'clock, and you compose yourself for sleep."

"That's all very well for you to say, Nurse," he pointed out. "But I'm a poor sleeper. Always have been. You know that. Listen. I'm paying ten dollars a day for this room, and care, of course. What difference does it make if I wish to read for an extra hour or two at night? Tell me that?"

"Do you believe that rules are necessary, Mr. Fletcher?" Alex asked. "You are a businessman—or were. How long would your business have run successfully without a system of some sort? A set of rules to be followed by your employees? It's the same with a hospital. Meals at certain times, TPR readings at a given time, visitors during certain hours, medications, baths, examinations at others. Lights out at nine."

"Okay, okay," he groaned, tossing his book to the table beside the bed. "You always make everything sound so reasonable and convincing while you are talking, but as soon as you leave the restrictions irk my free American spirit. I guess I'm hard to reform, my dear. I have always done about as I pleased and—"

Alex smiled into the faded eyes and patted the thin hand on the coverlet. "I know," she said softly. "You have done as you pleased, and see where it has brought you. Now you are paying for that self-indulgence. Sometimes Mother Nature is slow to punish her erring children, but sooner or later we are called upon to pay for breaking her rules. You are lucky in that you have a strong constitution, my friend. Everyone isn't so fortunate. Now close your eyes and think of the pleasantest experience you have ever had. Good night. Sweet and untroubled dreams."

"Good night, Nurse," he murmured, as she turned to leave the room. "I guess I need these nightly lectures." His light went out as she closed the door, and Alex sighed. The same thing every night. She should think he would get tired of it. She didn't hear the man's satisfied chuckle as he told himself that she had spent a few minutes with him anyway. Doctor Allen stopped her as she moved on down the corridor.

"How does the new job go, Blair?" he asked.

"All right," Alex answered, moving on to the next room.

"What's your hurry?" the young man wanted to know.

Alex paused briefly. "Did you want something, Doctor?" she asked cooly. "There are two vacant rooms on the fourth floor of this wing, but none of the third, Doctor Allen," she said.

"I'm not looking for a vacant room," he told her curtly as he strode away. So that was it. She was carrying a chip because of Mordock. Well, let her. He had been in the right, and if she had an ounce of brains she knew it.

Alex's head was high as she pushed open the door of the next room. The night superintendent turned as she entered. Bronson, the attending nurse, moved aside and

43

Alex went to stand beside the bed. It was plain to see that the woman lying there so white and still was close to death. Ridley's hand was on the pulse and her face was grave, almost frightened.

"Call Doctor Hammond, Blair," she said clearly but somewhat curtly.

But it was Bronson who left the room, and Alex asked quietly, "She's worse, isn't she? Where is Thompson?"

Ridley ignored the question.

"You should have reported her condition, Blair," she said.

"But she was better last night. Doctor Hammond—"

"Didn't you come to this room at once upon coming on duty, Blair?" the night superintendent demanded.

"Of course not. I came on duty at the usual time, and have been making routine visits ever since," Alex replied evenly.

"This is what comes—I warned Halliday," Ridley murmured.

"If you have any complaints perhaps it would be wise to consult Miss Halliday," Alex said stiffly. "Where is Thompson? Why isn't she on duty?"

"I discharged Thompson for impertinence, Blair," Ellen Ridley snapped.

"*You* discharged her! But what about the patient? Surely that was her prerogative."

"Are you daring to question my ethics, Blair?" the night superintendent demanded icily.

"Blair may not, but I certainly dare, Ridley," Doctor Hammond announced crisply as he entered. Doctor Allen was with him. Bronson followed.

"This is what comes of discharging her special." Alex heard Hammond growl. "Just because you didn't happen to like her. Bah! Get out. All of you!"

As the door closed behind them leaving the resident and Ellen Ridley inside, Alex heard no more. Douglas Allen turned and went back into the room. Alex wondered what was happening. Two doctors and the night superintendent but no nurse.

"She's too fresh," Bronson muttered vindictively. "I wish the Chief would fire her. She's no good here. Didn't like Vera Thompson, the special! That certainly is the limit."

44

The door reopened and Doctor Allen came out. He hurried down the long hall to the telephone, and Alex heard his exclamation of impatience. She waited until he returned.

"Is there anything I can do to help, Doctor?" she asked.

"If we need anything Bronson can take care of it," he replied coldly. "Thompson isn't available, and who can blame her?"

Alex moved on down the corridor to her next objective. It was growing late. Visitors were gone, and most of the rooms were dark, patients asleep. But occasionally a light shone faintly, and Alex walked softly to see if anything was needed. This floor was extra special. Only the very rich could afford rooms here. Back at her desk in the alcove, she saw Ellen Ridley come out of the room. She looked angry and went through the nearest exit with speed. Doctor Allen called Bronson whose eyebrows lifted whimsically as she passed Alex. It was almost an hour before she returned.

"Just what was it, Bronson?" Alex asked as the nurse sat down to make an entry on the Wilcox chart.

"Nervous chill, impeded circulation, and a bad case of jitters. The lady was so angry that she has actually retarded her recovery a solid week. That's what uncontrolled temper can do to a person, Blair," she went on. "Well, it took some doing to bring her back. Perhaps Ridley wasn't far wrong when she called her a neurotic introvert, but just the same, this is one time her ladyship pulled a boner, Blair."

There was a note of satisfaction in her usually placid voice.

"The Wilcox family aren't going to love her for this. It was certainly a dumb thing to do, letting one of her specials go, and I can't understand it. Ridley's smart enough, land knows, but you can't tell her anything. She knows it all. Why Lovell told me at dinner tonight that she had reported 314's condition earlier in the afternoon, and Ridley made light of it. Said she would be all right and that it wasn't up to the nurse to tell her when specials were needed and when superfluous. She did say though that she had an engagement that afternoon and would see the patient later. Off with Allen probably. I wonder just why she sent Thompson packing. And I wonder if it was real ability or pull that got Ridley through training. She's pretty, or don't you care for her type? And, of course, she is the Chief's granddaughter."

"She is very pretty, Bronson," Alex agreed.

"And she's man-crazy, too. Don't forget that. Do you think Allen and she will make a match of it, Blair?" the nurse went on. "I shall feel sorry for the lug who marries her. Allen's sort of a friendly guy, you know. I like him." She sighed deeply. Alex said nothing. She was trying to imagine just what had happened and what was occurring in the small operating room on the top floor. So she merely murmured a faint agreement, and went on with her thinking.

"How do you like being a supervisor, Blair?" Bronson continued, wishing the midnight lunch would arrive soon. She was growing sleepy and needed her coffee.

"Oh, it's all right, I suppose," Alex said without enthusiasm. "But I think I like straight nursing better."

"I do, too. No supervisor job for me, not that they ever asked me to take one, but if they did I shouldn't want it. But let me give you a tip, Blair," she went on, lowering her already low voice until it was merely a whisper. "Watch out for the two of them—Ridley and Allen. Not that I think Allen would do anything of his own volition, but that Ridley wouldn't stop at murder if it suited her purpose. I don't trust that one."

Alex giggled. "You've been reading too many horror yarns, Bronson," she jeered.

"No I haven't, but Ellen Ridley hated Ann Mordock, and if she thinks there's a chance of Doctor Allen falling for you, I wouldn't give two cents for either your job or your reputation. She's that sort, Blair. I know her type. Just because her grandfather, grand old chap, is Chief of Staff here, she's got the idea that she can do no wrong. She's crazy about Allen and she won't stand for any trespassing on her property—or what she thinks is her property."

"Of course you are talking the most utter nonsense, Bronson," Blair said somewhat sharply, "but she may rest assured as far as my ever being of the least interest to Doctor Allen or vice versa."

"Don't be so positive, young lady," the older nurse declared. "You've got it all over Ridley as far as looks are concerned, and besides that you're sweet and kind. We all ove you, we older members of the staff, and she knows it."

Alex put out her hand to the woman standing beside her desk, and said quietly, "Listen, Bronson, get all such thoughts out of your head. Ellen Ridley is absolutely no concern of mine. We seldom come in contact with each other. What she does or what she thinks interests me not at all. I am here as a nurse, just now as a supervisor, and nothing else matters. Forget whatever it is that is troubling you, and remember that we in the west wing have a standard of nursing to maintain. That's all that matters. Now I wonder what Mrs. Oliphant wants. I'll go, Bronson. You sit down and rest awhile. Sometimes it is pretty rugged going up here, isn't it? Lunch will be along in a few minutes. It is almost twelve forty-five."

Bronson sat down gratefully. Alex was like that, never sparing herself, but watching to see where she could ease the work of her nurses. "What do you think of the idea that Haddon Memorial nurses be equipped with roller skates, Blair? Think of the time we'd save, not to mention the wear and tear on the old pedal extremities. Wow!" she groaned. "Why, oh, why did I ever become a nurse?"

Alex hurried down the long hall to where a light flickered above the door of 327. She was smiling. Bronson was comical and, old as she was, she was one of the most dependable nurses in the entire hospital. She thoroughly resented Ellen Ridley, and made no bones about it. If the night superintendent realized it, it made no impression on her complete satisfaction with herself. Alex shrugged the thought aside. After all, it was none of her business. She was sorry if Ridley had pulled a boner, but after all she was supposed to be efficient and qualified to hold the position she did. She didn't like her, and was quite aware that the night superintendent felt no affection for her either. She pushed the door of 327 wider and entered the faintly lighted room. Mrs. Oliphant was sitting up in bed, her eyes wide with terror and, even as Alex entered, she let out a most unearthly scream and pulled the bed-clothes high above her head.

"Mrs. Oliphant!" Alex cried catching the woman's shoulders and holding them firmly in her two hands. "What on earth is the matter? Have you been dreaming

47

again? That's what comes of eating all that rich candy at night. I warned you what would happen."

The woman stared at her in disgust. "You warned me! You warned me!" she repeated. "What good was that? You should have confiscated the boxes and refused to let me have any. A fine place this is I must say!" She began to cry and clung to Alex's hand. "It was horrible. Horrible! I think I am going to be sick."

And for the next hour she was sick and kept Alex and the floor nurse busy, with Bronson the usual tower of strength. But after a time she felt more comfortable, and Bronson bathed and massaged her back, put on a clean nightgown and fresh bedding, and she lay back breathing quietly.

"I bet our coffee is cold, Blair," the older nurse complained as they left the room and moved toward the alcove and Alex's desk. There were no signs of lunch, and Bronson sputtered vindictively. "The snips!" she cried. "I bet they took them back. I'll just go down to that kitchen and tell them what I think of 'em," she stormed, marching toward the elevator.

"Don't do that, Bronson," Alex urged. "I'm sure there is some explanation. I'll call the kitchen and find out what happened."

"We have your lunch right here, Blair," a voice answered. "Ready for it? There was no one about when Blacky brought up the tray, and she waited awhile and heard a commotion in one of the rooms and thought you were all busy so she brought it back. We made fresh coffee and added an extra treat to your tray. Coming right up, dearie."

And it was there almost as soon as Alex returned to her desk. The treat was a thick slice of chocolate cake and real cream for their coffee.

"Maybe it pays to have something out of the ordinary happen up here," Bronson declared as she sipped the hot coffee. "Pretty decent of the gals to think of us, isn't it? Mmm this is good!"

CHAPTER SIX

IS IT THAT you don't like me, Blair, or just that you think it might be an infringement of one of Halliday's precious rules?" Doctor Allen asked as Alex refused his invitation to dine and dance on her next night off duty. "I know tomorrow is your free night. I made it my business to find out, so just why won't you go with me?"

"I expect to be busy during the afternoon and evening tomorrow, Doctor Allen," Alex pointed out.

"And it isn't due to either of the reasons I mentioned?" the young man persisted. "I'm glad to know that. That's one thing your being a supervisor allows you freedom in—to accept invitations from male members of the staff. I'm glad, too, that you don't actually dislike me. I was afraid you did. Oh, hello, Ellen," he said, his eyes staring at a point above Alex's bright head. "Where did you come from?"

Alex turned to encounter the cool blue gaze of Ellen Ridley. She took a step forward, and Douglas Allen laid a detaining hand on her arm. "Don't let me spoil your delightful tête-à-tête, Doctor," the night superintendent said scornfully. "Up to your old tricks, I see, flirting with the staff. Marie won't be pleased, will she, Blair?"

A wave of anger swept over Alex Blair for a moment. She saw the flush of resentment flood the young surgeon's good looking face. Quickly she turned to him. "Thank you, Doctor Allen," she said quietly, even a bit sweetly. "I shall enjoy accepting your invitation. Is there any particular time I should expect you?"

Douglas Allen caught her hand in his. "Thank you, Alex," he murmured. "I'll be around at six-thirty. It's my night off, too. We'll have ourselves a time. Don't worry about Miss Halliday, Ellen," he counseled the night superintendent. "It was partly due to her kindness that I managed to summon up enough nerve to ask Alex for a date. She's hard to get, you know, and I'm a bit shy."

"Shy! You? Don't make me laugh, Doug," Ellen Ridley said waspishly. "So Halliday's on your side. She would be, the—"

"Naughty, naughty!" Doctor Allen warned, shaking an admonishing finger at her. The door before which Ellen Ridley was standing closed, and the young man turned to grin boyishly at the girl before him. "Don't mind anything Ridley might say or do, Alex," he told her soothingly, for he saw the perturbed expression on her face.

"But she is probably right, Doctor," Alex murmured.

"Not that one. She is almost never right. The gal has

a whale of a lot to learn, and she's going to find the going mighty tough. Do you believe in corporal punishment, Alex?" he asked. "I mean the laying on of hands forcibly where punsihment is indicated?"

Alex smiled. "Do you by any chance mean spanking?"

"Spanking."

"Sometimes it is the only way to make an impression, I'm afraid," she answered. "Why?"

"Well, it is most unchivalrous, I know, but Ellen Ridley should have been thoroughly spanked on an average of twice a day during childhood—once before the act was committed, and again afterward on general principles. It would have saved her the theoretical spankings she's bound to get during her adult life. She has been shamefully spoiled. A great pity, too, for she has many fine qualities, I know, but she has been pretty much of a brat since she came here—taking advantage of the fact that her grandfather is Chief of Staff and one of the grandest men in the world. Don't let her bluff you. Don't let her think you are afraid of her. It would be fatal."

"I'm sure you exaggerate, Doctor," Alex said serenely. "And I assure you that Miss Ridley means nothing to me one way or another. I doubt if she could injure me in any way."

"There's where you're wrong, my dear," the young man told her a bit worriedly. "Ridley boasts that she always gets what she goes after. That sooner or later things have a way of coming around to her advantage, by clever maneuvering on her part, of course. And if she takes it into her head that you're not a proper supervisor, or if she wants the job for someone else, or if she simply wants to make trouble for you, she will leave no stone unturned to have you removed."

"Let her," Alex said shortly. "I'm not so sold on the job that it would break my heart to lose it. Don't worry about me, Doctor Allen. I assure you I can take care of myself." She moved quickly and silently away from him, and felt rather than saw his look of bewilderment. She entered the elevator and was carried to the fifth floor where Bailey and the floor nurse were in close conference at the desk in the alcove.

"I was about to page you, Blair," the older nurse said as Alex approached. "We're in something of a fix here.

'Old Sour—' Miss Milton refuses to stay in bed and after all you know, Blair, she's—"

"She's a patient here, and as such must obey the rules of the hospital in spite of her wealth and social prestige." Blair was walking noiselessly down the long, dimly lit corridor to the room occupied by the patient known to the staff as 'Old Sourpuss.' The room was rather cool at this time of the evening, and the patient in thin silk robe over her sheer nightgown (she absolutely refused to wear the hospital garb, even the special kind) was sitting on the edge of the bed, her bare feet swinging just above the floor. She looked grim, cold, very determined, and ready to fight for her rights—and Alex paused just inside the door before she spoke.

"I suppose those nosy nurses tattled on me," Miss Milton said sourly. "I hate tattletales. After all, I'm paying for this room and if I want to sit on the edge of my bed I shall do so, nurse or no nurse." She spoke with finality, and Alex acknowledged that perhaps there was something to be said for the woman. And yet, in her present physical condition, she should be lying flat with her feet well covered and resting quietly, even sleeping.

"But it is their job to keep me informed as to our patients' condition, Miss Milton," Alex pointed out reasonably. "Tell me, why do you want to sit up just now? Restless? Can't you sleep? Perhaps a glass of hot milk will help. Would you like that? Or a massage? Perhaps an alcohol rub or a hot water bottle at your feet?"

"I suppose if I told you that I want none of those things you will send for Doctor Hammond or some other man who thinks he knows it all. Well, I won't give Tom Hammond the satisfaction of poking fun at me again, so if you will give me that warm—not hot, mind you—milk and a hot—hot, mind you, not lukewarm—water bottle, I'll settle down and try to get some sleep in this boiler factory. Honestly, Miss Blair, this is absolutely the noisiest place I was ever in."

Alex opened her eyes in amazement. "Noisy? Here? Why we think the west wing here in Memorial the very quietest of places. Just what particular noise disturbs you, Miss Milton?"

"Listen. Don't you hear them? Noises. All sorts of noises. A kind of humming, buzzing all the time." The woman shook her head as if to rid it of the offending disturbance, and her eyes were wide with fright as they met those of the nurse. "You don't suppose I am losing my mind, do you?"

Alex smiled down at the anxious face, and shook her head. "We'll have Doctor Rose in tomorrow to examine your ears, Miss Milton. Do you know him? Well, he's the best otologist in these parts. Of course Doctor Mathews could examine you, but I feel sure he would advise having Doctor Rose. How long have you had these noises in your ears? I am quite sure that your trouble is there. Probably wax hardened. That is quite common and easily taken care of."

"You are such a comfort, Miss Blair," the patient sighed gratefully. "I have been troubled with head noises off and on for weeks now, but I disliked saying anything about them. You know, I'm old and sort of useless, and it would be easy to put me away—" Tears choked her and Alex smoothed back the gray hair from the thin face, and was glad when the floor nurse brought in a tray.

"Here's your warm milk, my dear, and a nice hot water bottle. Right?" She pulled a blanket about the thin shoulders and covered the cold feet, slipping the hot water bottle into the bed.

"Do you know, Miss Blair," the patient told Alex as she sipped the warm milk and snuggled in the comforting warmth of the blanket, "you're the best supervisor we have ever had in this hospital, and I should know. I hope they will never move you from this wing—not while I live, anyway." There was silence for a space while the milk slowly disappeared.

"All gone?" Alex asked as the patient placed the empty glass on the table beside her bed and slipped her feet between the warmed sheets. "Now you're going right to sleep and forget everything unpleasant. All right? Comfortable? Sweet dreams, Miss Milton!" She patted the well covered shoulder, and slipped out the door closing it softly behind her.

Bailey came down the corridor from the end room as Alex reached her desk. Morrison, the floor nurse, dropped into a chair beside her. Bailey grinned as she neared them.

"What a night this promises to be, Blair!" she muttered taking the chair on the other side. "Did 'Old Sour—,' I mean Milton, calm down any? How did you manage it? She abused me shamefully. Called me a fat old snail, and Morrison here an impudent young snip. If I were a sensitive creature I should have been insulted, but it takes more than that lady's remarks to faze me. How did you work the subjugation, Blair—as if I didn't know?"

"Oh, I guess she just felt rebellious for awhile, but it soon wore off. She was ready to surrender by the time I got there and was docile as a baby—agreed to everything I suggested. Poor old thing! She's lonely and the only way she can get attention is to start something like this. I feel sorry for her; terribly sorry. It must be hard to be old and alone in the world."

"Granted, but she's not the only lonely old woman, Blair. We have a good many here from time to time," Bailey pointed out. "With her money she could have plenty of company."

"I know," agreed Alex, "but paid companionship isn't quite like that of loved ones."

"Well, couldn't she grow to love someone?" Morrison asked. "They tell us that love begets love."

"Hmm," Bailey mused, pursing her lips. "She's not very lovable, that one. To attract love she would certainly have to mend her ways. The name 'Old Sourpuss' wasn't given her for nothing. She's got a vile disposition."

"Loneliness can do that to a person," Alex said.

"It hasn't made me sour," the older nurse retorted. "I have neither chick nor child, my parents died years ago, and my one brother was killed in World War I. I'm all stark alone in this unpredictable world, and yet I find life interesting, exciting, and oftentimes amusing in spite of people like Milton, Harkness, et al."

Alex smiled. "Ah, but you keep busy, my dear," she said affectionately. "You have plenty of inner resources that you can draw on from time to time. I doubt if you will ever be lonely, Bailey."

"I hope not," the older nurse answered sincerely. "I can always find something to keep me busy, mentally as well as physically. I guess my mother had the right idea when she instilled into my somewhat empty head the fact that Satan always finds mischief for idle hands, and much evil for idle heads."

Morrison yawned widely, patting her mouth with slim

53

fingers. "Gosh, Bailey, you make me tired just listening to you talking about all the work there is to do in the world. I'm looking forward to a time when I can just fold my hands and loaf, thinking of nothing and doing nothing. I'm perfectly willing to let you do the work, and you're quite welcome to any glory accruing from it. As for me, give me a life free from both labor and worry. I'll guarantee I'll never find it either lonesome or boring."

"Nonsense!" the other retorted. "You don't know what you're talking about. Believe me, you'd get mighty tired of loafing. We all get times when work doesn't appeal to us, but take it from me, it is God's perfect gift to man—the panacea for life's greatest disappointments and worst ills."

"Hear, hear!" applauded Alex softly, clapping her hands. "Truer words were never spoken. There's Sherwood's light, Bailey. Do you want to see what she wants? I'll take a look into 521, and then I must go back downstairs. I don't think there will be anything very disturbing tonight. If there should be, you can call me."

She walked swiftly and silently to the last room on the floor. It was occupied by Simon Clark, fast becoming a hypochondriac, certain that the stomach ulcer from which he suffered was instead a particularly malignant cancer. Alex pushed open the door of the dimly lighted room and stepped inside. The patient was staring fixedly at a spot just above his head, a look of sadness on his face. Alex took the cold hand lying outside the coverlet and pressed it gently.

"Are you in pain, Mr. Clark?" she asked softly. "Can I get you anything?"

The man shook his head hopelessly, not moving his gaze from the ceiling. "What's the use?" he murmured sadly. "Nothing will help."

"Are you in pain?" the nurse asked again.

"No. No pain," he answered. "It must be close to the end."

"Why do you torture yourself like this, Mr. Clark?" Alex asked. "Why don't you enjoy this respite from pain? You are much better, you know."

"You just say that to make me hope, Nurse," he told her morosely. "I know when I'm licked. The sands of time are running out and the absence of pain is a bad sign."

"A little knowledge is a dangerous thing, my friend," Alex said crisply. "Now I am going to give you a bit of advice—advice that my grandfather used to give me when I had been a naughty girl, which I assure you was quite often, and at bedtime I was almost afraid to go to sleep. Here it is, and you can take it for what it's worth which is plenty. He used to come into my room and would take my hand in his, like this, and then he would say quietly, 'Have you said your prayers, Lisa?'—he always called me Lisa. 'If you haven't then say your prayers, my dear, and close your eyes and be still. The rest will follow quite naturally.' It did, too, invariably. Try it, Mr. Clark."

She patted the hand and smiled into the man's anxious face. He made no reply, and she said nothing more, but left the room pulling to the door behind her. Did the poor fellow seem relieved? Comforted? She hoped so.

Everything was quiet all along that dim corridor and her rubber soled shoes made no sound on the polished floor as she walked its length to the elevator at the end. Downstairs quiet prevailed as well, and the three night nurses looked up to smile as she joined them at the desk midway of the long hall. It was eleven-thirty and she listened for a moment to reports on one or two cases, then went on down to the third floor where she once more came in contact with Ellen Ridley. The night superintendent greeted her coldly.

"I advise you to watch your step with Doug Allen, Blair," she said sharply, pausing before the young nurse. "He managed to lose your pal her job, and he is quite capable of doing the same to you. Just because you are a special pet of Halliday won't do you much good then. Out you'll go just as Mordock did. Take my advice and give him a wide berth."

"I suppose you think you are being kind, Miss Ridley," Alex said coolly, "or do you? I assure you I am quite capable of taking care of myself and my own affairs without help. Don't bother about me. How is Mrs. Wilcox this evening?"

The night superintendent stared suspiciously at her for a long moment, but Alex's face was bland. She didn't want to quarrel with this girl. Even while annoyed at her interference, Alex felt a little sorry for her. Somehow she sensed the unpleasant aggressiveness of the other was a pose to bolster her ego, and camouflage an inferiority complex. But that was a crazy idea.

"Oh, she's coming along," Ridley replied after a moment. "The poor creature has an overactive imagination. If she had less money she would have been relegated to a psychiatric hospital long ago but—you know how it is."

The subdued voice of the transmitter calling Ridley reached them. Alex listened. "Calling Superintendent Ridley. Calling Superintendent Ridley. Wanted in small o.r. at once. Calling Superintendent Ridley."

"Shut that thing off!" Ridley cried sharply to the floor nurse who hurried to close connection. The night superintendent showed no disposition to hurry. In fact her steps were leisurely as she walked along the hall to the stairs.

"Some day she is going to get hers," the floor nurse muttered vindictively, "and I don't mean maybe."

Bronson joined them. Alex asked about Mrs. Wilcox. Bronson reported that the Chief had taken over, reestablished her specials, and wouldn't allow his granddaughter in the room with her. "The woman hates the sight of her," the nurse said in an 'I told you so' tone of voice.

"But I had the impression Mrs. Wilcox was a special friend of hers," Alex said.

"*Was* is right," Bronson grinned. "She very definitely isn't any more. She insists the gal wanted to get rid of her."

"Nonsense!" Alex retorted sharply.

"No nonsense about it," the other said flatly. "It was a plain case of spite. Ridley fired one of her specials as unnecessary with no thought, apparently, of the fact that the general duty nurses in this wing are every one of them overworked and can devote only so much time to each patient. Spite has no place in a hospital—personal likes and dislikes either. Do you know, Blair," Bronson went on soberly, "it isn't the hard work connected with nursing, it isn't the uncooperative and grouchy patients we have to take care of, it isn't even the lack of appreciation and far from liberal financial remuneration accorded nurses—it isn't any of these things that sometimes make *us* sick and tired of our jobs and prevent girls from wanting to join our profession. No, Blair, it isn't any of these reasons. It's simply the stinkers—yes, stinkers who manage to worm their way into the profession—the plain, everyday stinkers who call themselves nurses and are a disgrace and shame to the rest of us. Women of the Ridley type—selfish, bossy and uncooperative. It's heartbreaking, Blair."

It was a long and involved tirade, and decidedly foreign to the mild nature of the elderly nurse. Alex laid an understanding hand on Bronson's shoulder. "I know," she said softly. "But you will find the same conditions in every profession. There are good and bad people in them all."

"I suppose so," Bronson conceded.

Alex looked in on Mrs. Wilcox and found the patient feeling very much better. Her lips were pink, and her eyes had lost their look of terror. She smiled as the young supervisor entered.

"I'm glad it's you, Miss Blair," she said, brushing her hand across her eyes. "If it had been Ellen Ridley I should have screamed. And to think she called herself my friend, Nurse! Friend? Fiend! That's my opinion. I hope Doctor Allen doesn't get into her clutches, that's all."

Alex smiled at the patient's vehemence and shook her head. "Don't be too hard on her, Mrs. Wilcox," she admonished. "After all, everyone is apt to make a mistake occasionally. Miss Ridley is a very clever young woman— really brilliant and an exceptional nurse."

"What right had she to discharge one of my specials? It was I who was paying her salary. I could have died. Yes, I could," as Alex smiled and shook her head. "Oh, I know she called me a neurotic introvert given to temperamental displays to gain attention. All I cay say is that she need not come around me any more. I'm afraid of her. I actually am. When am I going home, Nurse?"

"It won't be long now," Alex told her, and left the room. She had heard the persistent rumors about Ellen Ridley's infatuation for the assistant surgeon, but had taken it all with a grain of salt. In a place like this if a doctor showed the least interest in one of the nurses or vice versa, it must be love. In this case it might, of course, be true, but what about the report of the night superintendent's engagement to a Chicago man?

The more Alex thought about it, the less she liked the idea of going out with Doctor Allen. She had no desire to play second fiddle or to be the third side of any triangle. If the idea was to make Ridley jealous and so bring on a climax, she wanted no part in it. Just why had she accepted his invitation? She bit her lip and experienced a feeling of shame when she recalled that it was simply because of the night superintendent's possessive attitude and almost bossy manner. She wasn't proud of herself. What was she to do now? Could she manage a plausible excuse or should she keep the date? She continued on her round of calls, pushing the problem aside to be settled at some future time. And it was the superintendent who was responsible for the broken engagement after all.

For a time Alex wondered if perhaps Ridley had influenced Miss Halliday in changing the schedule that permitted Alex to have the evening free. But her common sense told her that the superintendent was by no means easy to manipulate—even by such an influential person as the Chief's granddaughter. If along with her relief at the broken date, she experienced a twinge of regret, she promptly shrugged it aside. Everything had worked out beautifully. Just as she had hoped it would.

CHAPTER SEVEN

AND ALEX WAS back in the west wing at the usual time, the date with Doctor Allen canceled. The young man was inclined to be angry when she called him to report that she was not to have the evening free as planned.

"But Halliday told me you were to be free, Blair," he complained. "I can't understand it. Are you sure you didn't do a bit of finangling—that you didn't really want to keep the date?" he said crossly. "I have everything planned—"

"I'm sorry, Doctor," the girl said not too truthfully "But you should realize the conditions here at Haddon. My relief is down with the flu. What can I do?"

"Oh, the west wing could get along without you for one measly night. You're too easy, Alex. Why didn't you tell Halliday that you couldn't work tonight?"

"You know better than to ask such a question, Doctor Allen. That's the way it is, and I'm sorry about your plans. No doubt someone else can take my place."

"I'm not worried on that score," he snapped. "It's only that I don't like being stood up."

"Don't be silly," Alex said sharply. "I'm not standing you up. I have to be on duty. I'm a nurse, Doctor Allen, just in case you may have forgotten."

"Oh, I'm not likely to forget," he answered, and slammed the receiver forcibly into its cradle.

"Too bad," a voice murmured at her elbow as Alex slowly replaced the instrument. "But don't take it too much to heart. I doubt if you would have enjoyed a date with Doug, anyway. He likes his women gay and responsive, and I doubt if you ever for one moment forget that you are a trained nurse—just now a night supervisor."

Alex remained standing with face averted while Ellen Ridley made her unpleasant speech. She was angry that the other had probably heard the conversation, or enough of it to imagine the rest. "Well, you can undoubtedly take over the date, Miss Ridley," Alex said quietly. "I'm sure that is what you want."

"Oh, Doug knew I already had a date," the other laughed without mirth. "But I'll say this for Doctor Allen, though, he certainly was brave to risk a date with one of the ice princesses. Of course you know that is your title among us more approachable humans." She began to walk away.

And Alex, suddenly appearing to find the whole affair amusing, said mirthfully, "Who are the others, Miss Ridley? The ice princesses, I mean. How very quaint!"

The night superintendent swung around and stared at the girl with something like admiration in her cool blue eyes. "There were only two of you, you know—you and Ann Mordock. Now you wear the title alone." She hurried away as if fearing a reply, but Alex, laughing aloud, went on to the elevator and about the business in hand which was to change from street clothes into uniform. Her simulated mirth was gone. In its stead was a feeling of resentment and almost disgust.

"What a cat Ellen Ridley is!" she said to herself as she slipped out of her coat and hung it in her closet. "And what a useless waste of ammunition! I'm sure I shall never be a rival for Douglas Allen's affections, nor for that of any other man blind enough to fall in love with her. I wonder just why she dislikes me so much. I have never done anything to her." She shook her head and went on with her dressing. It was nearly time for dinner and she was hungry. She hoped they were to have baked fish tonight. She was fond of fish, and being Friday it was the time for it.

Bailey greeted her as she reached the fifth floor some time later. She exclaimed in surprise, "What are you doing here, Blair? I understood you had a heavy date for tonight with our, or rather Ridley's, heart interest. Don't tell me the gal threw a wrench in the plans."

For a moment Alex felt like making a sharp retort but thought better of it. She knew that Bailey meant no offense; that she was interested, and that she was undoubtedly glad of any affront to the night superintendent whom she thoroughly disliked.

"Calhern is down with flu," Alex explained simply. "The date's off. Why?"

"Oh, nothing, only I don't trust that dame. It would be just like her to maneuver things so it fell through. Too bad, Blair. I think you would have enjoyed going out with Allen. He's a fine lad."

"I expect I shall survive," the girl said coolly. "Anything special up here, Bailey? Miss Halliday mentioned a new pneumonia case."

"Room 513, Blair," the nurse answered. "He's someone quite important, I take it from the fuss Hammond and Ridley made over him. His name is Grandon—Richard Grandon. Know anything about him? He's young— thirtyish, I should say. Tall and rather handsome. At least, Ridley said he was. I heard her telling Morrison about him. It sounded to me as if he might have been one of her beaus, but then she probably just imagined it or made it up out of whole cloth to impress Morrison. The girl was starry-eyed at the romance of it. Phooey!" Bailey sputtered. "I bet she doesn't even know him."

Alex laughed. "Forget it, Bailey," she advised.

"He's been taken care of for the night, but the resident is with him now. He has specials, of course. One of them is Mordock's cousin. Do you know her?"

"I've met her," Alex said. The door of 513 opened and Doctor Hammond came out. He came directly to the desk where Alex sat. She rose as he approached.

"Keep close watch on 513, Blair," he said making a

notation on a pad. "The nurse on duty will report to you from time to time, but I want you to satisfy yourself that the treatment we are using is working according to schedule. He's a pretty sick young man, Blair, and needs careful watching." He laid the pad on the desk and turned away. "Call me at the least change," he went on, "although it is early to expect any right away."

"Yes, Doctor," Alex answered, and picked up the pad to read of a medication to be administered in case the patient roused. "I believe I will take a look at him right now, Bailey," she said, slipping silently along the long hall. The door of 513 was closed and she opened it a bare crack to look in. Phyllis Mordock rose from her seat beside the bed and moved quickly to the door, finger on lip.

"Oh," she breathed, "It's you. I was afraid it was Ridley. She's a pest, hovering about bothering me. How's tricks, Alex? Seen Ann lately?"

Alex's eyes were on the bed where the patient was breathing heavily. His face was flushed and his eyes but partly closed.

"How is he doing?" she asked.

"Okay as far as we can tell right now," the nurse answered. "Here is his chart."

It was touch and go with Richard Grandon for severa days and nights, and when the fever abated and weak and languid he grew daily more irritable, his specials were worn to a frazzle and ready to give up. The lungs failed to clear as soon as anticipated and x-rays showed a rather serious infection in the right lung. In some way the patient discovered the result of those x-rays and immediately considered himself doomed. An unhealed spot on his lung meant ultimate death to him. At first his attitude was one of resignation, although at°times he was almost facetious only to lapse into unexpected gloom. All three of his special nurses found the going difficult, and there were times when Phyllis Mordock threatened to quit. It was due to Alex Blair's diplomacy, her understanding and tact, that the young nurse stayed on. But there were times when she was close to tears, and Alex had all she could do to ease the situation.

Ten days went by and a substitute was found to relieve Alex and, as if he had been waiting for just such an eventuality, Douglas Allen caught up with her when she reached the fifth floor of the west wing.

"I've heard it said that everything comes to him who knows how to wait," he greeted her. "So inasmuch as we both have tomorrow night off we can keep that long deferred date. Okay with you, Alex? I hope it is. I've been looking forward to it, and it appears to me that you could stand a change and a bit of fun."

And because Alex was tired and feeling decidedly seedy in spirit, she said she felt she would enjoy a binge of some sort.

"It has been a pretty strenuous time up here," she acknowledged. "But then it's like this every year during winter, and yet it's such a lovely section of the country that at other seasons we forget the hard winters."

He picked up a chart that lay on the desk and studied it for a moment. "Hmm," he murmured, after a moment. "Nick Appleton certainly made a quick turn in the right direction, didn't he?" He replaced the chart and grinned down at her. "I certainly hope nothing happens to spoil this date, Alex," he said whimsically. "There seems to be a jinx on my plans lately—if you believe in jinx. I'm glad you are to have this free time though. You need it. We work you pretty hard here in Haddon, Alex, and you are losing some of your color."

"I'm perfectly well, Doctor Allen," Alex assured him flushing at his critical gaze. "Of course, as I said before, it is always like this at this particular time of the year. February and March are tough in this climate, especially for the old and those with low vitality."

"I know," the young man agreed. "And this section is particularly bad for pulmonary affections—bronchitis, pneumonia, sinusitis and the common cold. I was warned of that when I came here, but it is such swell country that I decided to risk it."

"Risk it?" Alex asked. "But you are not predisposed to any of those diseases, are you?" wondering why he continued to linger, and wishing he would go on about his business. She knew both Bailey and Morrison were pointedly keeping out of sight.

"Oh, no, I'm a pretty healthy fellow. Hello, Doctor," he greeted the resident who came out of 513, followed by

Phyllis Mordock, the special, who motioned to Alex to join her.

"I was just going to call you, Doctor," the resident said shortly. "Harry Lang down in 417 insists he is getting up."

"Ridiculous!" Doctor Allen asserted crisply. "What ails the chap?" He turned as the two nurses went into 513. "Anything wrong there, Doctor?"

The resident shook his head. "Not a thing, only the boy's restless. Says he's sick of being coddled. I think he's scared. That bad right lung, you know. Blair'll fix him. She can always quiet these obstreperous ones. How she does it is one for the book. A great nurse, Doctor. I almost wish they had let her remain a general duty nurse instead of making a supervisor of her."

Doctor Allen stirred restlessly, and Hammond said, "Come on down to 417, Doctor. Perhaps you can talk turkey to Lang. If you can't make him understand the seriousness of his condition, maybe Blair can." The two doctors walked toward the elevator and disappeared.

Inside 513, Richard Grandon looked almost sulky as the nurses entered. "Well," he muttered huskily, "what do you expect to gain by reinforcements, Nurse?"

"Oh, I thought that perhaps Miss Blair could suggest something that might ease your restlessness." Alex thought the girl looked about ready to drop from fatigue and despair. Her eyes were very bright as if she were fighting tears.

"Are you a magician then, Miss Blair?" the young man asked witheringly. "If you are then for Heaven's sake help me to get out of here. I tell you I'm going nuts. I'm all right. What's a spot on a lung? It's nothing to make a fuss about. What's a cold?" It was said with bravado, but Alex knew he was worried and frightened.

"A cold you say?" Alex answered. "My dear man, you had a pretty tough bout with pneumonia, or won't you acknowledge it? Are you by any chance a disciple of the cult believing 'thinking makes it so'? If that is the case I can give you a formula—more of a ritual, really—that might help you as it has helped others." She smiled into the harassed dark eyes, and some of the dread modified.

"Okay, go ahead, shoot," he told her, settling back against his pillows to listen.

"This isn't a cure-all, mind you, nor is it mumbo jumbo to be repeated lightly. One must be relaxed and quiet and even receptive, if you know what I mean."

"That sounds as if you had tried it yourself," the young man said. "Have you?"

"I have never been ill enough to need it," the girl answered. "But I nursed someone who has and is using it now, and he says it is wonderful."

"All right, give me the lowdown on this formula or whatever it is. I am relaxed, quiet, and ready for any eventuality, as the saying is." He grinned, and Alex thought he seemed better. Then why had he been so uncooperative, so fussy and disagreeable that his nurse was discouraged?

"The first time I heard of this treatment for nervous and harassed patients was in connection with a young flier who was forced down near a small town where a friend of mine was nursing in the hospital. He was terribly wounded so that there was a question of his ever leaving the hospital alive, much less fly again. This friend of mine who was his nurse used to hear him murmuring over and over to himself certain words. At first she thought he might be delirious, and then gradually she made out the words. Something like this, 'God is a spirit, infinite, all powerful, changeless. I am a part of God's infinite plan, therefore, all is well with me. I am serene. I am not afraid, for day by day in every way I am getting better and better.' His eyes were closed, but over and over those whispered words came to her. They seemed to fill the whole room. After awhile he slept. His pulse and respiration improved. When the Chief of Staff stopped in to see him some time later, he was amazed to find him still alive. Not only was he alive, he was definitely better. In an unbelievably short time he recovered and left the hospital, and I know that today that man is perfectly well and back at the controls, flying one of the big transport planes."

The patient was lying quietly, his eyes fixed on the calm and lovely face of the young supervisor. "You make it sound like a miracle, or is it the hocus pocus of some cult one is constantly hearing about? I'm not a religious man, girls. I don't do much praying. I have always felt I could look out for myself, so why bother God."

"Listen, my friend," Alex said quietly. "A Haddon

nurse is not supposed to talk religion to her patients. There are ministers, rabbis and priests to do that on occasion, and they do it much better. This hospital is non-sectarian, but I am not talking religion, Mr. Grandon. I am merely advocating a soothing, quieting, strengthening ritual, or prayer if you like. After all, you no doubt learned the catechism when you were a child?"

The young man shook his head. "I didn't come from that kind of a home," he answered.

"You have missed a great deal then," Alex told him. "But one is never too old to begin, you know. Why not give it a trial right now?"

"I believe I will," he said simply. "Will you stay for awhile and coach me if I get the words wrong?"

"The words don't matter, Mr. Gordon," Alex told him gently. "It is the spirit, the desire, the yearning for comfort, the soul reaching out for help that counts. Don't worry about the exact words. Just relax and let your thoughts reach out into the Great Beyond." She nodded to Phyllis Mordock, and quietly withdrew. If the young man noticed her leaving he made no sound.

"Please God help him to find peace," she breathed as the door closed behind her.

She finished her round of calls and didn't see either Doctor Allen or the resident again that night. She ate her midnight lunch with the girls of the third floor and listened to more complaints of the night superintendent's interference. She wondered why the young woman went to the trouble of antagonizing the nurses the way she did. Or maybe she was quite unaware of doing so.

"Do you think she and Allen will make a match of it, Blair?" Bronson asked as she devoured the generous wedge of cake with which the tray was furnished. "He's a fool if he marries her. And tell me what she has that the rest of us lack? Oh, she's the Chief's granddaughter, and probably rich with lots of social advantages, but she's a cat for all that."

"Doctor Allen's nobody's fool, Bronson," the floor nurse pointed out. "He's been here less than four months remember. He's still looking us over, maybe," she laughed gleefully at the mere thought. "But take it from me, girls, he'll get his eyes open after awhile and then, bingo! I used to think he sort of liked Mordock until he got her fired.''

"Don't be ridiculous!" Alex said sharply. "That was purely a misunderstanding. Mordock is on leave and will be back almost any time now. I hope." The last two words were said to herself for she didn't know when or if Ann intended returning to Haddon.

"That's not the way I heard it," the floor nurse insisted, "but let it go. He isn't allowed to date mere nurses, I'm told—or, maybe it's the other way round—we're not allowed to date him." She giggled. "I'd risk it if he asked me for a date, the dragon notwithstanding."

"Did Mrs. Wilcox leave today, Bronson?" Alex asked, hoping to change the subject. "She was anxious to get home, I know."

"Her daughter came for her at five this afternoon, Lovell told me. Do you know, I liked that woman, Blair. Perhaps it was because neither of us could stand the night superintendent. Could be," she laughed.

Alex shook her head. She rose to her feet and hurried toward the elevator. She wished she could change the nurses' attitude toward Ellen Ridley. But there seemed only one way to avoid discussing her, and that was to leave.

"Will you be back right away, Blair?" the floor nurse asked. "Don't you want your cake? Thanks!" as Alex shook her head. "D'you know, Bronson," she said to the nurse beside her. "I know Blair doesn't like Ridley. How could she? And yet you can never get her to say a word against her. She won't even listen to what others say, either."

"That's all right, Tabby," Bronson said. "It would no doubt be better for us all if we followed her example. She's tops, Blair is, and don't you make any mistake about it. Douglas Allen is a blind fool."

"Hmm," the younger nurse muttered. "Maybe he's not such a fool as we think he is. Morrison told me he and Blair have a date for tomorrow night, Ridley willing."

"What do you mean, 'Ridley willing', Tabby? What has she to do with it, and are you sure?" Bronson sat bolt upright in her chair, her face avid.

Tabbert giggled. "You know how lawyers and ministers always say they will keep an appointment 'God willing'?

Well, instead of 'God', who I feel sure couldn't play a mean trick on anyone, I used the name of her nibs who has a most uncanny and diabolical way of cramping everyone's style. I wonder if she knows about this planned date? I hope she doesn't. Blair's got some fun coming to her."

"Do you know, Tabby, I don't think Blair likes being a supervisor. She loved general duty nursing."

"She should worry," the other replied. "If she were a mere general duty nurse, she couldn't have dates with Allen. So you see, my duck, there's no great loss without some compensating gain, or words to that effect. More power to her, say I!"

Some time later, and quite unaware of this eulogy, Alex walked the short distance from the hospital to the nurses' section with mixed feelings. She wondered what Ellen Ridley would have to say when and if she discovered about this date.

CHAPTER EIGHT

ALEX DRESSED with more than her usual care on the late afternoon of her date with Doctor Allen. She was annoyed with herself for feeling nervous and even a bit excited at the prospect. After all, she didn't really know Douglas Allen, and she asked herself why she was letting down the bars of her rigid reserve in this particular instance. Could it be that she wanted to show Ellen Ridley that her possessiveness of the young surgeon was merely temporary and not at all conclusive? She shook her head. She felt sure she was not that vindictvei. To be sure, she didn't like the night superintendent, and knew that the feeling of dislike was mutual, but even so, she was sure she bore no actual malice toward her. Then why was she giving up one of her rare and precious evenings for a date with a man she scarcely knew and had no intention of encouraging further? But she went on examining her wardrobe until she found just the proper frock she felt sure would be both appropriate and becoming.

On her way to the fifth floor where she was on duty, Bailey stopped in at Alex's room not only to satisfy her curiosity, but to tell her of the noticeable improvement in 513, young Grandon's condition. His special had told the floor nurse that the improvement extended to his disposition also. "She's a cute girl, isn't she?"

"You mean Phyllis Mordock? She is cute, and sweet as well. She adores her cousin, Ann, and wants her to go in for private work instead of staying on here at the hospital. But Ann doesn't care for private duty, she told me, and I shouldn't be surprised any day, or night, to see her back here."

"Will she get her old job back, Blair?" Bailey asked. Her tone was a little worried for she enjoyed working under Blair. "I like Ann but, well, I've gotten used to you."

"She can have the job and welcome," Alex said. "It was forced upon me, and I should be happy to relinquish it at any time."

"Well, one thing about being a supervisor is in your favor, Blair," the other pointed out. "Ordinary rules and regulations don't apply to you."

"How do you mean?" Alex asked. "I try to live up to the rules just as I always have. Being a supervisor hasn't changed that any."

"Oh, but it has," Bailey said. "You can now have dates with male members of the staff. The nursing contingent haven't that privilege, my dear."

Alex nodded. "I'm dumb, I suppose, but I never thought of it. And yet Doctor Allen pointed that out to me some time ago. But listen, Bailey, this date tonight doesn't establish a precedent. I don't intend making a practice of this sort of thing, and don't go letting your imagination work overtime. Understand?"

Bailey giggled, and Alex smiled at the older woman who was notoriously romantic.

"Well, have a wonderful time, Blair," she said as she left the room. "But I shall keep my fingers crossed so that Ridley won't put a jinx on the evening."

The door closed, and Alex frowned as she slipped into her frock, smoothing it down over slim hips and stepping back from the mirror to view the hemline—a feat not at all easy considering the size of the mirror. But she got a fair idea of the effect and began to feel a growing excitement as the hour approached. There was a faint knock on her door and, at her call to enter, the small maid stepped inside, her expression eager, her eyes wide with curiosity.

"Doctor Allen is downstairs, Miss Blair," the girl said in an awe-struck whisper. "He said to tell you to take your time but, well, he acted sort of excited. I thought he had made a mistake, and he nearly took my head off when I said of course he meant Miss Ridley." She giggled nervously. "Wasn't that awful of me, Miss Blair? But how was I to know? It has always been her, Miss Ridley before, and— Shall I tell him you'll be right down, Miss Blair?"

"Yes, Dora, you may tell him that." Alex ran a comb through her hair, smoothing a curl around a finger and slipping a hairpin through it to hold it in place. She pressed her lips firmly together for a moment, saw that her nose was not at all shiny, picked up her fur coat, tucked a filmy handkerchief of linen and lace into a pocket, took a final glance at herself in the mirror, and went slowly down the long three flights of stairs. She heard voices as she reached the lower hall, and paused for a moment wondering if perhaps the night superintendent was waiting, too. But she soon recognized the voice as that of Dora Drake, the maid, who was explaining between nervous giggles the reason why she had failed to understand that it was Miss Blair and not Miss Ridley he was taking out to dinner.

"I'm sorry I was so dumb, Doctor," she told him. "I promise I won't make that mistake next time, and honestly, Doctor, I'm glad you got your eyes open at last. That Ridley woman's a pill. None of us like her much."

"Tut, tut, child!" the young man chided. "Haven't you been taught not to criticize those in power?"

Another giggle, and the girl answered. "It's a free country, Doctor, and I always say what I think."

"A very unwise habit; a dangerous habit," he pointed out. "It is quite apt to get you into trouble if it hasn't already."

"Who cares?" Dora answered indifferently. "This isn't much of a job anyway, and it wouldn't break my heart if I did get fired."

Alex walked into the room, and Douglas Allen rose to his feet and bowed ceremoniously. "Thank you, Dora," he said, dismissing the maid. "I shall overlook your mistake this time, but be sure you never repeat it."

"I promise, Doctor. Cross my heart and hope to die," Dora giggled and winked at Alex. She hastened to open the front door for them, and stood watching while the young surgeon helped Alex into his small green car. It was not until they had disappeared down the driveway that she closed the door and sighed deeply. A voice summoned her to the kitchen, and she scurried along the hall and was soon wiping dishes to the accompaniment of an elaborate and purely imaginary account of an infatuated Doctor Allen and a starry-eyed Alex Blair as they kept the first of a long line of future dates.

"Stop it, Dora!" Mrs. Martin warned sharply. "And if I ever hear of your carrying such tales to the rest of the house I shall—well, I shall do something drastic. Do you understand?"

" 'Drastic,' Mis' Martin?" Dora wanted to know. "What's that? Do you mean you'll fire me?"

"I hope it won't come to that, Dora," the housemother said. "But we don't like gossip here, you know. And besides, Miss Blair is one of our very finest nurses—sweet, kind and capable. I wouldn't have her hurt for anything in the world."

"Gosh, Mis' Martin," the girl exclaimed in horror, "I wouldn't hurt her! I like Miss Blair. She's okay." She laid down a plate and stood for a moment hands on hips, eyes belligerent, head thrown back and lips pursed. "But if I ever get the chance to take that Ridley down a peg, believe me I'll do it if it costs me my job or a leg. I hate that woman, Mis' Martin. How I hate her!"

"Now, now, Dora!" Mrs. Martin rebuked. "What has the night superintendent ever done to you that you should dislike her?"

"Done to me? She's treated me like dirt and pushed me around, that's what she's done. Told me to clean two pairs of white shoes and take her raincoat to the cleaners over on MacDougal Street and wait for it. Imagine! Anyone would think she was my boss; that I was working for her. And did she pay me extra for all this? She did not. Not one red cent. Why, Mis' Martin, she even had the nerve to tell me I must have dawdled when I didn't get back as soon as she thought I ought to. And when I told her I had other work to do besides waiting on her, she told me I was im—impertinent. Did she report me, Mis' Martin?"

Mrs. Martin shook her head. "No. This is the first I have heard of any of this, Dora. But don't worry. I understand she will be leaving very soon now."

"How soon?" the girl demanded, reaching for another

plate and wiping it vigorously. "How soon, for heaven's sake?"

"Two or three months, I imagine."

"Call that soon? I'd like to kick her out this very night." She giggled reminiscently. "Won't she be burned up when she finds out about Allen and Blair, though! I'd give a good deal to see her face when she hears about it." She threw down the towel and did a little jig in the middle of the kitchen floor. "If I was there I'd laugh right in her face."

The night was cold and white with a sliver of moon and millions of stars in the deep blue of a late winter sky. The country through which the small green car traveled seemed already settled for the night, and the stillness broken only by the soft purring of the motor, communicated itself to the two inside. Alex found herself relaxing, and stole a glance at the man beside her. His face was serene and, even as she looked, his lips quirked in a smile.

"I wish you would pinch me, Alex," he said whimsically.

"Pinch you?" the girl asked. "Why? Sleepy? But why did you insist upon tonight then?"

"Sleepy? Me, sleepy? When I'm having a date with you? Don't be foolish, Alex," he replied. "It's that I can't make myself believe that you are actually here beside me, sitting in my unromantic old jalopy. Go ahead, Alex, go on and pinch me." He moved a shoulder a bit closer.

"Don't be silly," Alex told him. "Where are we going, or is it to be a surprise? I really don't know too much about places of amusement around here."

"They serve pretty good meals at the Chimney Corner out this road about fifteen or eighteen miles. Fairly good orchestra, too. It's popular, so I made reservations as soon as I knew I could count on you. You're such an unpredictable girl, one can't ever be sure."

"It's only that I am inclined to take my job seriously, Doctor Allen," the girl pointed out.

"Couldn't you make it 'Douglas', Alex?" he asked. "Just for tonight," he qualified, fearful of crowding his luck.

Alex hesitated then said simply, "I—I'll try, Doc—Douglas." She laughed, and the young man turned his head in astonishment.

71

"Do you know that is the first time I have ever heard you laugh, Alex," he said. "You should do it oftener. You have a delightful laugh!"

"Thank you," she answered demurely. "I haven't found too many things to laugh at or about in this job," she told him. "But I suppose one should not allow one's self to become too sober and sedate even amid tragedy and sorrow, sickness and pain such as we meet daily."

"Let me see," the young man mused. "You are about twenty-two or three—not more than twenty-three, I should say. Tell me just why you should become sedate at your age. I am not prying, Alex, and if you think it is none of my business, don't hesitate to tell me so."

"A few years ago I suffered a double tragedy, Doc— Douglas," Alex said quietly. "I was eighteen at the time. A double tragedy did I say? No, it was a triple blow and I nearly went under."

"I'm sorry," was all Doctor Allen said and comforting, sympathetic silence settled again on the occupants of the green coupe. On and on purred the small car winding up the miles beneath its wheels.

"There, just ahead is the famous Chimney Corner, and from the cars parked around it I imagine we shall have plenty of company," Doctor Allen announced. "I'll park over there on the left. Here we are, Alex. Wait on the porch for me. I won't be a minute."

Alex stood in the deep porch of the long stone and timber farmhouse with its huge chimneys and brilliantly lighted windows. From inside came the sound of music, and even here in the open but sheltered porch there was a general air of warmth and hospitality. Alex felt she was going to enjoy this evening away from the hospital.

Alex followed the hovering maid to the powder and dressing room and disposed of her coat. There were several girls and women before the mirrors and Alex merely used the small glass in her compact to assure herself she was all right before joining Doctor Allen in the hall outside. The dining room was well filled, but the waiter found their table which was not far from the huge glowing fireplace and offering a fine view of the room with its interesting floor-show and delightful orchestra.

"Comfortable?" Doctor Allen asked. "I think we have a good place, don't you?"

"Wonderful." Alex rewarded him. "I like it here. O-oh! No, no!" she breathed.

"What's the matter?" the doctor asked, as Alex's face paled, her eyes tragic.

Alex bit her lips. "It—it's nothing," she answered.

A young man came toward them and, smiling in pleased surprise, held out his hand to Alex. "Lisa. Lisa Blair! This *is* a happy surprise, Lisa!" he cried, taking the girl's cold hand in both of his. "How long have you been in Haddon?"

Alex answered with difficulty. Her throat felt full and her heart pounded dully. "I—I have been here four, no, five years, Jim," she said slowly, then turning to Doctor Allen she asked, "Have you met Doctor Everts, Doctor Allen?"

Douglas Allen grinned at the tall young newcomer, and they shook hands with enthusiasm. "I'll say I know him," he replied warmly. "Jim and I were in pre-med, and later did special work at Johns Hopkins."

"Why don't you two join Miss Ridley and me? Or have you other plans, and we might be butting in?"

Alex's hands were icy and, as she clutched them together, a little prayer for courage welled up in her heart. "Please make him go away," she begged. "Please don't let Douglas accept his invitation." And as if he felt her trepidation, the young surgeon shook his head.

"Run along, Doctor," he advised the intruder. "Our plans for the evening are complete, and don't include a foursome. I'll see you before you leave town, Jim," he went on, his eyes on Alex's face to which the color was returning.

"Oh, I shall be here for a day or two, Doug," the other answered. "I'm here as consultant on that amnesia case over in Saint Luke's." He turned to Alex again. "I hope to see you before I leave, Lisa," he said. "How about tomorrow sometime? Four, perhaps? Or could you have dinner with me later?"

"The afternoon would be better," the girl replied. "I go on duty at seven. Good-bye, Jim. Nice—" She didn't finish the sentence and the young man went back to his table, a puzzled expression on his pleasant face. He decided not to mention any of this to Ellen Ridley, and sat down in his place.

But he reckoned without Ellen Ridley's curiosity. She had often wondered about Alex Blair. The other girls prattled about home and family, boasted of them, received boxes of goodies from time to time—but never Alex Blair. She appeared to be quite alone in the world, and it wasn't natural. Her inquiries brought no information, and now as she watched this meeting and noted the girl's frightened manner, her curiosity increased. Just what was there to it? She would find out. Suppose Blair had a past—suppose there was something there the girl wanted to hide. Douglas Allen couldn't afford to be mixed up in anything remotely approaching a scandal, and somehow she had a hunch there was, perhaps, a scandal in the mysterious past of this particular ice princess. She frankly confessed that she hoped there was, and for a moment knew a twinge of shame. However, she was merely playfully curious as she smiled at her escort.

"And what a surprise that you should know our ice princess, Doctor!" she laughed.

"Ice princess? Is that what you call Lisa Blair? That's funny. That's extremely funny. Why Lisa is one of the warmest-hearted girls I know. Eager, active, athletic and popular—leader in the younger set of her home town."

"Her home town, Doctor?" the young woman asked. "And where might that be? You see, I am sort of a stranger here myself, having come from the Middle West. She's lovely, isn't she?"

The young man's gaze was across the room on the girl he had met so unexpectedly, and he murmured almost absently, "Yes, she is lovely." He let it go at that, and it wasn't until Ellen Ridley repeated her question that he appeared to wake from his daydreaming.

"What is it you called her—Lisa? We at Haddon know her as Alex. And where is this home town, Doctor? In this state?"

The young man nodded. For some strange reason he was reluctant to say more, and the young woman facing him frowned. "Hmm," she mused aloud, "a mystery. Incognito. Perhaps a real princess. What have we here? Come on, Doctor," she prodded playfully, "just who is Alex or Lisa Blair? And do you know, now that I hear it again, that name sort of rings a bell in my memory." She made a stab in the dark. "Wasn't there some sort of scandal, oh, not directly of course—but wasn't she connected in some way with something unsavory? Seems to me I heard or read something—"

"Nonsense!" Doctor Everts answered almost curtly. "Her name is Elizabeth but we always called her Lisa. Perhaps Alex is her first name, I wouldn't know. I have known her for years. A grand girl, and if you have heard of any scandal it certainly isn't connected with *her*. Not the girl I know. I wonder—"

"You wonder what?" Ellen Ridley asked. She felt she wasn't getting very far in this investigation. "I have wondered myself just why she came to Haddon, and who and what she is. She seems to have few friends except for a girl—a nurse doing private duty while on leave from our hospital. Ann Mordock? Know her, Doctor? Another ice princess. We have two of them. Especially blessed, are we not?" She smiled as she asked, but Jim Everts detected something very like spite in her tone. "Oh, they are both wonderful nurses, Doctor, but almost too good to be true—she and Alex or Lisa Blair are the perfect nurses, heard about but so seldom seen." She laughed merrily as if she found the entire affair merely amusing, but she didn't quite put it across, and she knew it.

Doctor Everts was sorry his meeting with Lisa had occurred here in this place and at this particular time. He had admired Ellen Ridley and had looked forward to seeing a good deal of her during this trip to Haddon, but suddenly he felt he didn't fancy the idea of ever seeing her again. And Lisa Blair had done this to him. Lisa who had turned him down for Phil Matson. He wondered just what had come between them—surely not the scandal and tragedy surrounding her brother Pete's death. He hadn't seen Phil in years. He wondered if his own recovery from that hopeless love was as complete as he had thought. He wondered too, why no one in Valary seemed to know where Lisa was or what she was doing. Well, he would keep her secret. He still cared enough for that.

"Let me see," Ellen murmured a bit acidly, "weren't we supposed to do some dancing here, Doctor, or was your meeting with an old girl friend too upsetting? I am quite willing to call the date off, if you like," she told him. She lifted a hand in a barely perceptible greeting to a group of

75

people passing their table. "Look, Doctor, I can join these friends and leave you free to continue your—"

"Nonsense!" Doctor Everts said again, interrupting his guest quite unceremoniously. "You will do nothing of the kind. I'm sorry for being such a bore, Miss Ridley," he went on apologetically. "Come, let us go. I believe the dancing is on the next floor, isn't it?"

They passed the table at which Alex and Douglas Allen were still seated, and paused while Ellen Ridley greeted them briefly and almost cordially. The eyes of the two young men met for an instant, and Doctor Everts slowly winked as he followed his guest from the room. Douglas Allen sat down and leaned across the table.

"Let's get your coat and go somewhere less crowded, Alex," he said whimsically. "There's a good orchestra over at the Plymouth House five or six miles north of here. How about it?"

"Not on my account, Douglas," Alex answered, feeling suddenly that this was all much ado about nothing. She felt sure that Jim Everts would do no gossiping about her to Ellen Ridley and anyway, what did it matter? It was all very much in the past.

"Just the same, I think we'll leave," the young man insisted. "Somehow I don't feel like sharing you with anyone tonight. This is our first date. and I don't want it shortened by so much as a minute."

They finished their dinner and Alex went for her coat. Her heart was warmed by the thoughtfulness of this man whom she had hitherto considered conceited and smug. Why, he was nice. She liked him a lot, and suddenly wondered if she was being disloyal to Ann Mordock. It was because of him that Ann had quit her job as supervisor. She was quiet as they sped along the snowy country highway.

"I'm sorry this had to happen, Alex," the young man said after a silence that seemed unbreakable.

"Oh, it was inevitable," Alex replied.

"He was in love with you, wasn't he? Jim Everts, I mean."

"We were both very young. He just thought he was. I have always liked Jim Everts, Douglas. He is a fine man."

"*You* might have been young at the time, Alex, but

Jim Everts is as old as I am—he must be six or seven years older than you."

"Well then, *I* was very young. I don't remember just how old."

"It is never too late, is it?" he went on.

"If you mean he is still in love with me, you are badly mistaken, Doctor Allen," Alex answered stiffly, "and I assure you it is the very farthest thing from my mind. I intend spending my life nursing the sick. It's a promise. Love is not for me and never can be."

"Now you are talking rubbish, Alex," he told her, "but maybe it is just as well that you feel like that at present. Now take my own case. I'm poor as Job's turkey and before I could even think of marriage, I shall have to finish here. I have a two-year contract, or what serves as a contract—an understanding, anyway—and then I want to take over a practice somewhere either in a small town or in the country. I want and need space in which to work. General practice and surgery with research on the side."

Alex laughed, suddenly feeling relief from the strain under which she had been laboring since meeting Jim Everts. "You are planning a wide and varied program, Doctor. Any one of those projects is a full time job."

"Yes, but I'm sure I can handle all three, Alex, especially if I get the right location and the right girl to help. But of course that is all in the future, and here we are—very much in the present. Not so many cars in this place, but I like it nearly as well."

And Alex was glad they had made the change for the music was good and the floor excellent and not too crowded. She relaxed visibly, and Douglas Allen's confidence increased as she laughed more and more often, and fitted into his arms as if she were quite at home there. She had been worth waiting for, he told himself. He had been attracted to Ann Mordock and even to Ellen Ridley, but in the first case he had suffered a revulsion when Ann failed to realize his position, and with Ellen Ridley he saw almost at once that she was not for him. Now, however, he experienced a feeling of satisfaction, contentment, oneness. This girl was the one with whom he hoped to spend the rest of his life. But he realized he would have to move slowly and carefully. Alex Blair was not to be rushed. She would have to be wooed gently. She had evidently suffered

77

a deep and terrible shock. Just what it was he didn't know, but he felt sure he could make her forget—could, as time went on, help in the healing of that wound, and could make her completely happy. A large order he knew, but somehow tonight, for the first time, he felt strong and confident that success would crown his efforts.

CHAPTER NINE

JUST WHAT DO you know about Alex Blair, Miss Halliday?" the Chief's granddaughter demanded next morning, making it a point to find the superintendent in her private office and alone. "Haddon Memorial has always been a stickler for background, character, and all the rest of it, and yet no one seems to know much of anything about Alex Blair except, of course, that she is pretty, if one admires her type, and appears to be an excellent nurse."

"May I ask what it is you want to know about her and why?" the superintendent asked cautiously. "Her application with the necessary credentials is on file. Your grandfather, Doctor Mathews, passed on it; the Board of Managers gave it their unqualified approval, and I, myself, saw nothing to disqualify her. You may see the file if you care to."

Ellen Ridley waved a negligent hand. "It is of no moment," she said. "I merely wanted to know the name of her home town, where she came from, and possibly the name of her sponsor. I suppose she had one. Do you know that, Miss Halliday?"

"Of course," Miss Halliday replied. "Mrs. Bigelow. Eleanor Whitcomb Bigelow, an alumnus of Haddon Memorial, and herself one of our finest nurses, sponsored her. Let me see, I think Blair was born in New York City, is an orphan, and at the time of her application was eighteen years old."

"Oh!" the young woman murmured. And the superintendent was wickedly pleased that she appeared disappointed. Ellen Ridley turned to leave the room, then paused to ask, "Do you know her full name?"

"Of course. It is Alexandra Elizabeth Blair. A most dignified name for such a small girl, isn't it?"

"Thank you," the visitor said, and departed, leaving the superintendent puzzled.

Miss Halliday didn't trust Ellen Ridley, and felt sure

she was up to some mischief or at least to no good. "Now I wonder why this sudden interest in Blair?" she asked herself, and reached into a filing cabinet for the folder containing the information she had given the questioner. Blair was evidently alone in the world. Such a lovely girl, too. She hoped the night superintendent wouldn't stir up anything. She was quite capable of it. Her lips became stern and her eyes cold. She would be glad when this spoiled granddaughter of the Chief should decide to marry and leave Haddon Memorial. She was constantly making trouble—criticizing, antagonizing, altering rules and schedules to suit her fancy, and upsetting the usually mild disposition of her grandfather, the Chief of Staff.

Down in the basement laboratory, Douglas Allen had been examining the culture taken from the throat of a suspected streptococcus meningitidis. He had about finished, and was scrubbing his hands preparatory to reporting his conclusions, when Ellen Ridley entered. She greeted him blithely, and once again Doctor Allen thought she had somehow just missed being beautiful.

"Hello, Doug!" she said, leaning against the cabinet near where he stood. "What became of you last night? You should have stayed."

"Oh, we went over to the Plymouth House out on the Turnpike. Good crowd and fine music." He finished drying his hands and drew down the sleeves of his white coat. "What's on your mind this morning?" he asked, not because he cared particularly, but for something to say.

"Nothing much," she replied negligently. "I was just thinking how next to impossible it is to quite bury one's past, to live down a scandal, or even to out-maneuver gossip."

Doctor Allen swung around and stared at her in simulated amazement. "Good heavens, girl!" he exclaimed. "Don't tell me people have found out where you hid the body of your victim after all these years! Too bad, Ellen, but you should have thought of that before committing the crime," he jeered. "You should have known even then that crime does not pay!" He covered his face with his hands in exaggerated distress for her plight. He was thinking fast. This girl had something up her sleeve.

"Very, very funny!" the young woman snapped, her eyes almost green in their anger.

"Did I guess wrong?" he asked with deceptive meekness, although he surmised what was in the mind of this almost beautiful girl. "Maybe you haven't been found out yet. But don't worry, Ellen, I shall keep your dark and dreadful secret. Wild horses cannot drag it from me. The profession must protect its secondary members. You are safe as far as I am concerned but, my poor deluded creature, you must watch your step in the future."

The hands of the woman opposite clenched in fury, and for a moment Douglas Allen thought she might even strike him. "Stop it!" she cried. "I'm talking about your new girl friend. What do you know about her? Doctor Everts called her Lisa. Here she is known as Alex. Why the disguise? What has she to hide? Who are her people?"

And although Doctor Allen was angry and disgusted at this inquisition, he managed to laugh derisively. "What is this?" he demanded. "What business is it of yours, and where do you get all that stuff about a purple past or a scandal? Shame on you, Ellen Ridley!" he jibed. "That's no way for a registered nurse—a bachelor of science—to act. Have you forgotten your oath? The sainted Nightingale is likely to turn over in her grave at your behavior it is so unethical. My, my!" Then seriously, "You were with Jim Everts last night. Why didn't you ask him? Or did you?" he continued shrewdly.

"Thank you for nothing," the irate young woman answered, as she rushed from the room. "Grandfather shall hear of this. The Board of Managers shall hear of this. There is something fishy about the sainted ice princess whom, against our combined advice, Halliday promoted to be night supervisor in the west wing. Remember, my fickle friend, you were as much opposed to that promotion as I was. I intend getting to the bottom of this, Douglas Allen, and maybe you'll be sorry you ever got mixed up with her."

Doctor Allen strode after the angry girl and caught her shoulder in a firm grasp. "Listen to me, Ellen Ridley," he said sharply, his voice low and menacing, "you lay off Alex Blair. If I hear of you so much as whispering a word of scandal about her, I shall make it my business to thoroughly cramp your style—you'll get out of this hospital so fast your head will spin, and your grandfather won't have a thing to say about it."

"Take your hands off me, Doctor Allen!" she stormed. "How dare you threaten me? Grandfather shall hear of this, too. I won't stand for it. Nor for a nurse who is hiding here and using the hospital for protection against possible deserved punishment for some crime she doesn't dare face," she raged, letting her imagination have full sway. "As for you, Douglas Allen, you had better watch your own step. Your position here is none too secure, I'll have you know." She turned her back on him and raced up the stairs, and feeling sure it would thoroughly annoy her, the young man managed to send a chuckle of amusement after her.

But he was far from amused, and made up his mind to have a talk with Jim Everts whom he had always liked. Was it possible Jim had gossiped about Alex, and reopened a closed and painful chapter in the girl's life? One thing of which he was certain was that Alex or Lisa Blair was blameless. She was incapable of evil in any form, and he would stake his life on that. But just what could Jim have told Ellen Ridley? How he detested that girl! He returned to the laboratory and, for some reason, washed his hands a second time.

Doctor Jim Everts called at the nurses' section at four that afternoon, and once again Dora Drake climbed the stairs to Alex's room to tell her a man was asking for her. Her eyes were glowing with interest, and her plain little face flushed with curiosity.

"My, but you're popular all of a sudden," she said admiringly. "He's not as handsome as Doctor Allen, Miss Blair, but he looks awfully nice. It must be grand to have two doctors simply mad about you. Aren't you thrilled, Miss Blair? I just wish that Ridley hag could see you now, Miss Blair. You look swell, so stylish and sort of snappy."

Alex laughed. "Don't imagine things, Dora," she told the waiting maid. "Doctor Everts and I are old friends. I have known him for years. He is very nice. I think he is a friend of Miss Ridley's, too, and I know that he and Doctor Allen were in medical school together. So you see, there is really nothing to get excited over. I'll go right down, and thank you for coming to tell me." She reached into the top drawer of her dresser for a chiffon scarf and held it out to the girl. "And here is something I want you to have, Dora. You have been very sweet to me, and I appreciate it."

"Oh, Miss Blair!" the girl exclaimed pressing the bit of loveliness against her cheek. "I always loved that scarf. Are you sure you want me to have it?"

"Of course," Alex replied. "I have intended giving it to you before, but just didn't get the chance. I hope you will enjoy wearing it, my dear. Now I must run."

Doctor Everts stood before one of the big front windows, staring out at the bleak landscape. His car stood at the curb, and he wondered if perhaps Alex, or Lisa as he knew her, might go out with him. He turned as she spoke from the doorway.

"Hello, Jim!" she said cordially. "It is good to see you again. Let me see, it must be five or six years, isn't it?"

"Five years and four months," he told her. "I was just now thinking of it. I was pretty hard hit when you decided to marry Matson, although I suppose I should have been prepared. Phil had everything and I almost nothing. I even came from the wrong side of town." He laughed as he spoke and there was no bitterness in it. What bitterness there once had was long since disappeared. "But time is a great leveler they tell me. Anyway, it has healing properties. How have you been, Lisa?"

"Very well, Jim," the girl replied. "Of course it was all pretty terrible, and for a time I thought I couldn't go on, but, as you say, time heals and I have now reached the point where the past seems much like a bad and unreal dream. Some day I shall go back to Valary, but not just now. I doubt if I am strong enough yet."

"The girls—your old crowd miss you, Lisa. I ran into Ann Simms—Ann Firth she is now, she tells me— and we lunched in Millie's Luncheonette. Remember that place? It hasn't changed any. After all, Lisa, everything that happened, or rather nothing that happened at that time was your fault or anything you could help. It was terrible. It was tragic, I grant you, but after all—well, your friends in Valary feel you should have stayed and lived it down."

Alex shook her head. "I couldn't endure their pity, Jim. Not even their sympathy, although I am sure most of it would have been sincere. No, I had to get out. Get away where I was not known, where people on seeing me wouldn't shudder or whisper and point me out as Peter Blair's sister. Not that I am ashamed of our relationship, Jim. I adored Pete. He was a grand brother, but he never grew up. He was a crazy, irresponsible, spoiled boy. But I shall never believe for one moment that he was bad. Pete couldn't be bad any more than Grandfather Blair could be evil."

"But nursing, Lisa?" Jim continued. "Why nursing? Surely you could have chosen a much easier line of work."

"I wanted hard work. I had to have it. And you know there was no money, Jim. After everything was settled there was practically nothing left. I had to find a job, and nursing seemed to be the answer. You see, Doctor Whitcomb has a sister who is a nurse, and I went to her until I straightened things out in my own mind. She's a wonderful woman. She manages a rest home in the mountains, and it was she who sponsored me when I applied here for training. Perhaps it was cowardly of me to extract a promise from Doctor Whitcomb to keep my whereabouts secret, but I felt that I had to find myself and rebuild my life as best I could, and I had to do it alone. You do understand, Jim?" she asked.

The young man nodded and pressed her hand. "I have always thought you quite wonderful, Lisa, and never more so than here and now. Your secret is safe with me, my dear. Are you happy in your work, Lisa? Do you like it here at Haddon? You know, probably, that Doug Allen and I are friends of long standing? He is a fine man—clever and honest, clean and of unquestioned integrity. If he is your friend, Lisa, you are lucky." He paused for a moment then went on almost hesitantly, "How well do you know Ellen Ridley, Lisa?" he asked.

"Our night superintendent?" Alex smiled. "I don't think I know her at all, Jim, why? She is beautiful, isn't she? Do you like her a lot?"

The young man shook his head, his expression dubious. "I, too, thought she was very beautiful, Lisa," he told her. "And I even thought I might fall in love with her but— don't antagonize her, Lisa. I believe she is dangerous or might very easily become so."

"Why are you telling me this, Jim?" the girl asked curiously.

"Oh, she was too interested, too prying about you;

jumped on the fact that I called you Lisa and here you were known as Alex. And by the way, where does the Alex come in anyway?"

"My first name is Alexandra, and when I signed my application I quite naturally wrote my full name. I have never liked it, but here nearly everyone calls me Blair, you see, so I didn't mind too much. Just what did you tell Miss Ridley, Jim?" she asked.

"Nothing," he replied, "and the lady didn't like my evasiveness. But I had a hunch that the less I said about you the better. However, my advice to you is to give the inquisitive Miss Ellen Ridley a wide berth. She told me you were dubbed one of the ice princesses, Lisa. I should like to meet the other one. I'm intrigued. Is she at all like you? Do you know her?"

"Of course," Alex answered. "She is one of the loveliest girls I have ever known. I am proud to be classed in the same category as Ann Mordock, and I shall make it my business to bring you two together if for no other reason than to take away the taste Ellen Ridley apparently left in your mind. When are you leaving, Jim? Maybe I can fix up something for tomorrow afternoon. Ann and I have tea together occasionally. Could you make it at three or three-thirty tomorrow afternoon?"

The young man laughed. "What is this, Lisa? Don't tell me you have gone in for matchmaking. But I shall certainly try to keep that date with you, blind though it is."

"Have no fear on that score, Jim," Alex laughed. "Dollars to doughnuts you will fall head over heels on sight. I adore her. She is my best friend—the only real friend I have here. Oh, I shouldn't say that, Jim, for I have many friends, but Ann is something extra special. Wait until you see her and you will understand, I'm sure."

"Say no more, my dear," he told her as she rose to her feet preparatory to leaving the room. "You make me almost afraid to meet this paragon. I wonder what she will think of me, Lisa. You know I'm just a struggling young doctor whose patients are conspicuous by their lack of appreciation of my quite remarkable ability. But my toes are on the first round of the ladder, Lisa, and while the climb won't be either spectacular or rapid, it will be at least steady and honest all the way up. I'm so glad for this little visit, Lisa. I have thought and wondered and, yes, worried about you a very great deal in the years that have passed. You see, I have heard nothing. Somehow everything pertaining to you was a closed and sealed book. No one knew anything. It hasn't been a happy time for me, or for any of us who knew and loved you. You have become even more beautiful, just as I predicted you would." He held her hands in a firm warm clasp as they walked to the hall, and Alex smiled to see Dora Drake scurrying up from the kitchen in order to open the door for him. The girl must have been hovering about the lower hall during the visitor's entire stay.

"You look happy, Miss Blair," the girl said when the door closed upon the tall young doctor. "He must be pretty special. But I like Doctor Allen better for you."

"Neither one is for me, Dora," Alex said severely.

"That's what they all say," the girl answered, and scurried back to the kitchen in answer to Mrs. Martin's insistent call.

Alex went on up to her room. She felt unaccountably happy. It was good to have had this brief contact with the past. What a fine person Jim Everts was! And yet she had rejected him in favor of a poor unstable reed, posing as a man, who had failed her utterly when she so sorely needed someone to understand and to help. And yet she felt no bitterness toward her erstwhile fiance—only scorn at herself for failing to see how weak and untrustworthy he was. Dear Jim! He was sweet, and she was glad to know that he was Doctor Allen's friend. She smiled to herself as she changed into uniform. She must get in touch with Ann and try to make a date for tea tomorrow afternoon. Ann was just the girl for Jim Everts. She hurried downstairs to the telephone to make sure Ann would be free.

CHAPTER TEN

ALEX WAS ASTONISHED, therefore, when just before she left for her tea date with Ann Mordock, the night superintendent came to her room in the nurses' section. She was looking particularly attractive, and seemed friendlier than usual. Alex was dressed for the street, but she asked her visitor to sit down.

"Are you going out, Blair?" the newcomer asked.

"Yes, but I can wait a few minutes. Was there something you wanted to see me about, Miss Ridley?"

"It's purely a personal matter, Blair," she said, and Alex saw that she appeared somewhat nervous. "You see, I have a feeling that you don't like me," she went on, "and I dislike having the enmity or aversion of anyone, especially one I admire as much as I admire you, Alex. I thought perhaps we might come to some sort of understanding; become more friendly. How about it? Can you tell me why you don't like me? I wish you would be perfectly frank about it. I am older than you, and I should be able to take criticism."

Alex smiled. "I can't imagine what you are driving at, Miss Ridley," she said evenly. "But I assure you my liking or disliking you should give you no concern. We have so little in common, and come in contact so seldom. And I am sure it isn't my place to criticize you," she went on, trying to arrange her thoughts, and to overcome the feeling of distrust for this woman's sudden desire for friendship. "But really, Miss Ridley," she said, a bit ruefully, "I doubt if we could ever be friends. Perhaps I am not a very friendly person, and I am sure that you and I are both far too busy to make the effort especially if it means much social activity. Would you mind telling me what you had in mind? What brought this on, for I am frank to confess I don't understand it in the least."

Ellen Ridley bit her lip, but she managed a tinkling laugh—that laugh that so often made people turn to look at her admiringly—and said, her voice dubious, "I have put it all very badly, Blair. You know by this time that I am, as Doug Allen says, a spoiled brat. But it is due to my upbringing, I suppose. I dislike being crossed or double-crossed and believe me, my dear, I have suffered a good deal of both. I know I have a vile temper, but I am honest about it. I am loyal to my friends, even while I thoroughly despise my enemies—and I assure you I am not an enemy to be taken lightly."

Alex laughed as she reached for her coat. This conversation had better come to a close. "Is that a warning, Miss Ridley?" she asked. "And just how does it apply to me? While I shall probably never be classed as a friend, I certainly am not and never shall be your enemy. I'm sorry if you are concerned about our relationship, and I assure you, you need have no least anxiety about it for I shall not. After all, life is too short to bear malice, and I am far too busy to waste my time and energy worrying whether people like me or not. I'm afraid I shall have to ask you to excuse me. I have an appointment and am late as it is." She stood aside to let the older woman leave the room ahead of her, and closed the door behind them.

Ellen Ridley left her without another word, and Alex had the feeling that she was far from pleased with the result of the conference. But what else could she have done? She still did not like the night superintendent, and felt she never could. They were worlds apart.

Alex hurried away from the hospital and out into the snowy street, her thoughts veering away from, then returning to the late disagreeable encounter. Something must have happened. Perhaps her grandfather, the Chief, had been talking to her, or maybe Douglas Allen. Perhaps she even hoped to curry favor with Jim Everts through her. She didn't know and frowned, frankly puzzled over the matter. During the more than a year and a half Ellen Ridley had been night superintendent at Haddon Memorial, she had made no bones of her dislike of her and Ann Mordock. She had not only pointedly ignored them as individuals, but had even gone out of her way to underrate them and disparage them to the rest of the staff. Both she and Ann had been quite aware of this, and after the first week or two it had bothered them not at all. Why, then, this sudden bid for favor? This offer of friendship? Alex shook her head in bewilderment.

Doctor Everts met her halfway to the tearoom where she was to meet her friend. How good it was to see someone from home! Alex hadn't realized just how much she had missed them all. They walked briskly along in the cold February afternoon, chatting animatedly and having a very good time. They reached the tearoom all too soon, and went inside where Ann was already waiting. She came forward, then paused when she saw Alex's companion.

"This is Doctor Everts, Ann," Alex greeted the older girl. "He and I were friends back in the old days before I ever thought of becoming a nurse. I want you two to be friends. You are both so very wonderful that I am sure you will be. Oh, I'm sorry, Jim. Ann is Miss Mordock, a former nurse in Haddon, and just now doing private work. When are you coming back to the hospital, Ann?" she asked, as they seated themselves at a small table close to the glowing fire. "We miss you, and I want to hand you back the job I have been holding for you."

Ann Mordock laughed and shook her head. "I doubt if I shall ever be a supervisor again, Alex," she answered ruefully. "Miss Halliday will never forgive me for running out on her."

"Don't be silly," Alex said. "The hospital needs you. We are full to capacity. How is Mrs. Brixton, Ann?"

"Fine. She doesn't need a nurse, although she insists that she does. I could come back tomorrow if—well, would Miss Halliday welcome me do you think?"

"Indeed she would," Alex assured her. "And do you think Ann here qualifies as an ice princess, Jim?" she asked the interested young man.

"As much as you, yourself, qualify as such, Lisa," he answered.

Ann looked from one to the other, her expression mystified.

"Didn't you know that's what the staff calls us, Ann?" Alex explained. "Or at least a part of the staff do."

Ann Mordock shook her head. "But why?" she wanted to know.

"You tell her, Jim," Alex said, nibbling cinnamon toast.

Jim frowned at her. "That's not fair, Lisa," he countered. "I'm a stranger here and not in a position to pass judgment. I was merely told that you two gals were known to the staff of Haddon Memorial as the ice princesses because of your reserve and, as my informant told me, the fact that you were 'almost too good to be true—excellent nurses, the sort one hears about but seldom if ever sees.' End of quotation. And now meeting you, I can quite believe the description applies, although I fail to see just why anything as cold as ice should be applied to either of you. There, my friends, that is a long and flowery speech for one as simple and prosaic as James Allison Everts, M.D. But I am glad to meet you, Miss Mordock—Ann," he went on boyishly, "and I am glad indeed that you and Lisa, here, are friends."

"Lisa?" Ann repeated.

"We at home knew her as Lisa Blair. Here, I understand, she is Alex. And I don't like it. How come, my dear?" although he had already been told.

"Oh, it happened quite naturally, Jim. I signed my application with my full name, of course, and when it was shortened to Alex, I just let it ride. I am known as Blair in the hospital, anyway, and so it didn't matter, really."

"It was good to see Lisa again," the young man went on. "I wasn't at all sure where she had located. But with friends like you and Doug Allen, Ann, I am sure she is happy and safe."

"Safe?" Ann asked.

"Safe from loneliness and boredom," he explained.

Alex laughed. "I have little time for boredom these days, Jim," she told him. "We nurses at Haddon lead strenuous lives, especially these days of the nurse shortage."

"I imagine it is the same everywhere. Somehow these days girls seem to shy away from anything that promises hard work. Hospitals all over the country are coming to depend more and more on aides and practical nurses. Too bad, too, because the R.N. has a definite place that no other less prepared girl can possibly fill."

A heated discussion followed as to the relative values of the various training schedules, and time flew while outside the day darkened, the wind increased, and a fresh blanket of snow covered the countryside. Ann looked from the window and exclaimed in consternation.

"Do you realize what time it is, good people?" She pointed outside, her eyes on her watch. "Nearly five. And I should be back by five. Don't let me break up this interesting discussion, but I will have to run." She held out her hand to the young physician who retained it while he insisted on walking her back to her job. Ann demurred, her eyes on Alex's smiling face. "Oh, all right," she agreed, "but it is not at all necessary."

"It is to me," the young man murmured.

Alex walked on ahead. She was smiling happily. Everything had worked out just as she had hoped it would. Ann was a darling and Jim Everts was everything a girl could possibly want in a friend, she told herself.

Back at the hospital some time later she came face to face with Ellen Ridley. The night superintendent stopped her with an imperious gesture.

"I don't want you to get the impression that I am

in the habit of proffering my friendship lightly to every Tom, Dick and Harry, Blair," she said coolly. "And what is more, I have no desire to force it on anyone. So, please forget my unwelcome visit to your room this afternoon. I assure you I shall not trouble you again." She turned and walked with her usual arrogance down the long bare corridor and into the waiting elevator.

Alex stood for a moment too astonished to move while the elevator dropped from sight, and it was then that Doctor Allen came from room 317 in which the patient had but yesterday suffered a cystotomy, and was still far from comfortable. He smiled when he saw Alex, who would have gone on about her duties, but he laid a detaining hand on her arm.

"Jim Everts tells me you had a tea date with him this afternoon, Alex," he said almost accusingly. "Why wasn't I invited?"

"The tea was really for Ann Mordock and me, Doctor Allen," she explained seriously. "Doctor Everts just happened along."

"That's not the way I heard it," the young man teased. Bronson came around the bend in the corridor, and then ducked quickly into the floor kitchen. Alex felt herself flushing and was annoyed.

"Well, that's the way it was," she said coolly. "How is 317 this evening, Doctor?"

The young surgeon's hand dropped to his side, and his expression became almost grim. "About as we expected," he answered shortly. He took a step away from her, then turned back. "What have I done now, for heaven's sake?"

"Done?" Alex asked, puzzled and showing it.

"You have changed, frozen up, shoved me back to where I was in prehistoric times. What happened, Alex? Ridley?"

Alex shook her head. "I haven't changed a bit, Doctor. Only I happen to be on duty now and— Oh, I can't seem to mix the social and professional as easily as apparently you can. First and foremost, I am a nurse, Doctor Allen, and you should be able to realize that."

"I didn't hear the whole of that tirade, Alex," the young man said happily. "All I heard was that you hadn't changed a bit—from last evening, I take it. We'll let it go at that. See you later. Have a good night!" He turned and hurried away, leaving Alex more bewildered than ever.

What ailed the people in this hospital? First Ellen Ridley, and now Douglas Allen. Bronson poked her head from the door of the kitchen and, seeing that Alex was alone, came out into the hall.

"Did you have a good time last night, Blair?" she asked interestedly. "It does my heart good to see you on friendly terms with Allen. He's a prince, Blair, and I should hate to see him continue making a fool of himself over Ridley. You're more his type, if you will pardon my saying so."

"I won't, Bronson," Alex said shortly. "Can't you girls get it through your heads that it doesn't mean a thing just because a doctor appears friendly with a nurse? Think back over all the doctors, internes and nurses you have known, Bronson," she went on coolly. "How many of them married? Not more than two or three, I'll wager. So get all that nonsense out of your head. Romance is the farthest thing from my mind, and I am sure it is from his, too. Now tell me if there have been any changes here."

"Nothing but what you already know," the older nurse answered, quite unoffended. "Ridley was up here shooting off her mouth and parading the authority she thinks she has. But we don't pay any attention to her. The worst case we have here on this floor is 317, but he has a special so we can pass him up. I never happened to know this special of his, Blair. Her name is Ainsley. Ruth Ainsley, she said. Seems a quiet sort. Burke told me the day special is a snip. But Burke hasn't much use for specials, anyway."

"I'll just run in for a minute," Alex said.

"Okay, you do that," Bronson replied. And Alex shoved open the door of 317 and looked in. Ainsley, the night special came over to her, chart in hand.

"Did you want something?" she asked softly, her eyes on the patient.

Alex shook her head. "I like to drop in on patients in this wing from time to time when I can do so without disturbing them. How is he?"

"About the same," the nurse answered. "Oh," she went on sensing the quiet authority of the other. "You're the night supervisor. I didn't know. You weren't here when I came on duty. Miss Ridley—"

"I have charge of three floors in this wing, Ainsley. Probably I was busy elsewhere," Alex explained.

"Three floors!" exclaimed the other. "How do you stand it?"

"Oh, it isn't so hard. This is a small wing, and not too many beds. Our staff is exceptional which helps considerably. I don't mind it. In fact I rather enjoy it."

"You're welcome to it," Ainsley told her. "Miss Ridley is the night superintendent, she told me. Over the entire hospital. Some job!"

"Yes," Alex agreed. "Hers is a real job, and I think she must be good at it."

Ainsley laughed and started to say something smart, but instead said, "Doctor Allen did this cystotomy, and a grand job it was. He seems to be a clever surgeon?" It was a question and Alex nodded. The patient was breathing quietly, his chart showed nothing out of the ordinary, and Alex slipped out.

The third floor was quiet, and she took the elevator to the fourth and found that, too, was under complete control with most of the patients quiet or asleep. The fifth floor, however, showed signs of activity, and Bailey held her head when she saw Alex leave the elevator. Morrison, too, looked relieved.

"What's the matter?" Alex asked as she reached her desk in the alcove.

"Specials!" groaned both nurses in unison.

"We have two new pneumonia cases here, Blair," Bailey told her, "and believe it or not we have three specials cluttering up the place. I wish they were anywhere else. They cause more trouble than a dozen of our regular girls. And do they demand service! Wow! 'Nurse,'" she called softly in falsetto, "'bring me alcohol, rubbing alcohol of course, stupid,' although I had no intention of bringing any other kind. Then it's 'Nurse, another pillow. Make it two. I must have help here.' I hate specials, Blair. What do they think we are, anyway? Why don't they get what they want themselves? They're getting paid for it, and we have work to do and can't spend all our time acting as maids to them."

"Of course not, Bailey. You should have showed them where everything was kept just as soon as they came on duty," Alex explained.

"I didn't get the chance. Her nibs, Ridley, was Johnny-on-the-spot and took complete charge of everything. That gal gets around, Blair."

"She certainly does," Alex agreed wondering just what the night superintendent's idea was. "Is this—which special is this coming now?" she asked as a tall young woman came swiftly and silently toward them.

"I need a dressing tray," she announced crisply as she reached the desk. "Bring it to 511 immediately."

"Let me see," Alex said quietly, "you are a special on duty in room 511? You will find everything necessary for a dressing tray in the cabinet directly behind you. Didn't Miss Ridley acquaint you with conditions here and show you where everything is kept? She should have."

"Well, hardly," the nurse answered haughtily.

"I happen to be night supervisor in this wing, er, is it Simmons? Oh, she is the special in 519. Then you must be Walker. I'm sure you will have no trouble assembling the ingredients you may need, Walker." She turned to Bailey who was showing her approval of Alex's handling of the disliked specials. "Has 509's cough eased under the new treatment? She must not be told there is codeine in that expectorant. You put it in a plain bottle? But of course you did."

"Bravo!" Bailey applauded softly as the special hastened back to her patient with the required tray, her head high and her back straighter than usual. "I wish I had your technique, Blair. Somehow they scare me, and they know it and take advantage. Wait until Simmons barges in here and demands orange juice, malted milk, and hot ovaltine. I know darned well 519 doesn't drink all that. Mmm, here comes the other one. Larkin. She's the worst." But as it happened she was merely in search of a hot water bottle, and was easily directed to the proper source.

She paused at the desk on her return with the desired utensil and said, her manner almost servile, "You are Miss Blair, the night supervisor, aren't you? Miss Ridley told me about you. I am happy to know you. You supervisors have it pretty soft here at Haddon," she went on, still in that soft ingratiating voice. "But of course Haddon is just a second rate institution. Miss Ridley was telling me the hard time she has been having trying to incorporate more modern ideas here. Too bad she has encountered so much opposition. Now at Saint Luke's and General the supervisors are always on hand with instructions even before specials arrive for duty. Miss Ridley has been trying to change that, but without much luck, she told me. Well, one can't teach an old dog new tricks, they tell us." She laughed at her own wit, and turned away. Alex said nothing. She had never before understood the reason for the enmity between general duty nurses and specials. Now she thought she knew, and didn't wonder.

Simmons made her demands a few minutes later, and once again Alex was ready with instructions. Simmons didn't see why Bailey, or Morrison, or even Blair, herself, couldn't help her by bringing her the things she needed without making it necessary for her to get them herself. Didn't they understand that she was on special duty? But after Alex had pointed out the impossibility of the two general duty nurses doing more than they already did, Simmons saw the light, and graciously condescended to take full charge of the patient she was engaged to nurse.

And all this turmoil and lack of systematic cooperation can be laid at Ellen Ridley's door, Alex told herself as she made ready to prepare the special medications for certain of the patients on the fifth floor. She wished she knew just what her scheme was and what she expected to gain by it. But soon she was too busy to think about it and it wasn't until much later that she felt repercussions.

CHAPTER ELEVEN

JUST WHAT ARE *you* expected to do at the spring dance and bazaar, Blair?" Bailey asked one blustery March afternoon, as the two sat in Alex's room and watched the wind roistering its way up the wide thoroughfare outside the hospital. "Her nibs, the Chief's granddaughter, asked to borrow my Paisley shawl. I hate like sin to lend it, but I didn't dare refuse. She wants to use it as a drape in back of the booth she expects to glorify by her presence. She seems to be bossing the entire affair."

Alex laughed. Bailey's outspoken dislike of the night superintendent always amused her. "Why did you let her have it if you feel like that, Bailey?" she asked.

"Oh, she was so sweet and persuasive, telling me it was the most perfect shawl of its kind she had ever seen and promising to be very careful of it. She'd better be or

I'll have her scalp." She returned to her first question. "Just what will *you* be donating to the affair, Blair?"

"I haven't heard," Alex answered. "Of course, there are the things in that box on the window seat that I have been collecting for the novelty booth. By the way, Bailey, who is in charge of that booth. Do you know?"

"I heard that Mrs. Widmer—Doctor Widmer's wife —is to have charge of novelties, and our own Mrs. Martin is to handle sandwiches, cake and coffee. I think Ridley's to have charge of the ice cream, with Doctor Allen's help." She made a wry face. "You don't have to ask who will do the work, Blair."

Alex refused to be drawn, and said, "Perhaps I shall be on duty and won't be able to attend at all. It will no doubt extend well into the evening, won't it? Then in that case of course I can't be there. Why? Are you going? And what are your duties?"

"Believe it or not, Blair," Bailey answered frowning. "I haven't been asked to handle the money—tickets that are purchased on the spot, and the result of the sale of ice cream, cake, sandwiches, and all the doodabs that have been donated for sale in the various booths. Just why I was chosen is a mystery to me. I'm no financial wizard nor a CPA either. Ridley told me I was to have a booth to myself and that everything would be brought to me. She assured me it was a very important job and a compliment to my ability. Phooey! Do you know, Blair, I don't think I care for the job."

"Why don't they get one of the men for it?" Alex asked. "It seems to me it is a man's job. What fun will you have sitting there in a booth holding the bag, so to speak?"

"That's just what I think, and I'm not going to do it," Bailey said emphatically. "Let her nibs get one of her beaus to do it. I'm lending my one and only heirloom and that ought to be enough. Anyway, if you work I shall work, too."

"Of course we are night nurses," Alex pointed out. "We may be able to take in part of the afternoon bazaar even if we can't attend the dance in the evening. I hope they won't ask me to do anything. It's years since I had anything to do with a bazaar. Last year I didn't even get to go at all, and while I was in training I didn't spend too

95

much time at them. I don't blame you for not wanting the treasurer's booth, Bailey, and if you work on that night you can't. Get out of it if they'll let you, my dear. It's a thankless job at best."

"And don't I know it. Ridley didn't fool me one bit by all that palaver about me being so dependable. That one missed the mark when she took me for an idiot. I may not be the world's cleverest nurse, but I sure know my Ridleys—and how! Believe me, I know when I'm being taken for a ride," the older nurse muttered disgustedly. She got to her feet and started for the door. "I'm going to hunt up that hussy this very minute and resign."

The door closed after her, and Alex frowned. She would be glad when the bazaar was over. She opened the box of things she had been collecting during the past weeks and months, and wondered if they would be considered worthwhile. Probably not by the night superintendent if she actually was running the affair, but she had thought them acceptable while she was buying them. Handkerchiefs, scarfs, a few doilies, children's socks, a set of antimacassars she had picked up at the Christmas sale her own church had sponsored, two rather loud neckties, and a half dozen guest towels. She felt it was a goodly assortment and repacked the articles and replaced the cover. The affair was to be held in the gymnasium here at Haddon Memorial, and she would ask Mrs. Martin to take care of it for her, as she felt certain in her own mind that she would not be attending.

It was perhaps two days later that Miss Halliday called her into her office. "Sit down, Blair," the superintendent said, picking up her fountain pen and tapping the desk blotter. "I am in something of a quandary," she went on after a moment. "Mordock has signified her desire to return to us, and I am wondering whether she should be reinstated as supervisor in the west wing or assigned to other duties. You have proved yourself perfectly satisfactory in the capacity of night supervisor and it wouldn't be fair to you to displace you. Have you any suggestions, Blair?"

Alex was surprised. When had the efficient and stern Halliday accepted advice or listened to suggestions from members of the nursing staff? Now, however, Alex spoke quickly and sincerely.

"I shall be happy to give way to Ann, Miss Halliday,"
she assured her. "You know I prefer general duty nursing
and always have, and I accepted the position of night supervisor at your request and not because I wanted it. I shall
be glad to go back to general duty work and am happy to
know Ann Mordock is coming back to us. She is a grand
girl, Miss Halliday, and a splendid supervisor." It was a
long speech for Alex, and Miss Halliday seemed, for a
moment, quite impressed.

However it passed almost at once and she said coldly,
"Understand, please, Mordock did not ask to be reinstated,
Blair. After all, she acted most unwisely in leaving us as
she did. It was thoughtless and, if I may use the term,
vindictive. She had committed a grave breach of ethics and
should have been willing to accept a well merited reprimand. But, on the other hand, efficient, well-trained, I
should say Haddon-trained nurses, are scarce and we need
her. So, beginning tomorrow night you will no longer be
night supervisor in the west wing. You will be notified
later just what and where your duties will be. That is all,
Blair, and thank you for your cooperation."

Alex left the room somewhat bewildered. It was
almost as if she was being censured. She had been perfectly
willing to step aside for Ann, and yet she had the feeling
that she, too, had committed a breach of ethics in saying so.
As if waiting for her to leave the superintendent's office,
Ellen Ridley, a look of satisfaction on her face, went in.
Alex turned in time to hear the door close, but didn't see
who the newcomer might be. She went on up to her room
and changed into a fresh uniform. It was there that Bailey
found her a few minutes later.

"What's this I hear about your being demoted, Blair?"
she demanded sharply. "Don't tell me that Halliday's
under Ridley's thumb, too. I heard her tell that snippy
special on the Barkley case that she was planning a change
in the west wing. *She* was planning a change, mind you.
She intimated an older woman—not me, I assure you—was
to have the job. Do you know anything about it, Blair?"

"I don't suppose it is any secret, Bailey," Alex told
her. "But I am going back on general duty after tonight,
and Ann Mordock is coming back as night supervisor in my
place. She isn't old though, is she?"

"What'll you bet she doesn't get the job, Blair?" the

older nurse said positively. "I have an idea Ridley will throw a wrench in that plan of Halliday's. Did you know that Ridley was at the bottom of this shift, Blair?" she asked worriedly.

Alex shook her head. "If she is, I'm sure she isn't aware she is doing me a kindness in giving me back my old job, Bailey," she said. "For if she is, I think she would have worked it another way."

Bailey said nothing for a long moment, her expression one of deep concern. "Doctor Allen and she aren't such good friends as they were, Blair," she said meditatively. "You should see the dirty looks that pass between them when they happen to meet. And yet she told me that Allen was to help her dispense ice cream and soft drinks in her booth at the bazaar. Maybe she just thinks he is. I bet the guy has no idea of the honor she is about to bestow on him."

Alex didn't answer at once. It was all very puzzling. She didn't even know to which part of the hospital she would be assigned. Was this the night superintendent's method of retaliation—of punishing her for refusing her phony offer of friendship? She sighed. She had found her life in Haddon Memorial quite uncomplicated until now. Just why should it have suddenly become so difficult?

"You haven't been out with Doctor Allen lately have you, Blair?" Bailey asked. "Of course it is none of my business and I'm not being nosy, but all this could stem from his interest in you."

"Nonsense, Bailey!" Alex answered shortly. "I doubt if Miss Ridley had anything to do with this change. Certaintly she wouldn't have been in favor of bringing Ann back. Or would she?"

"Don't be too sure that Mordock will get the job, Blair," Bailey said pessimistically. "That woman's a fiend. I shall be glad when she gets out of here. If she ever does. I wonder if she really is engaged to be married. I pity the man. It will be heavenly when she leaves, and I'm not alone in that opinion. Somehow I have a notion that Doctor Allen will be the happiest of us all—unless it's the gal's long-suffering grandfather. I wonder just who Bruce might be. Does the name mean anything to you, Blair?"

"Bruce? Bruce who?"

"Bruce. That's all I heard. The Chief told her she'd

better give up this farce she was playing and go back home and marry Bruce. Of course I wasn't supposed to be listening, but the Chief was angry and didn't lower his voice. Ridley didn't answer him. She just rushed off evidently intent on more mischief." The nurse sighed deeply.

Alex smiled. "Don't take it so to heart, Bailey," she said soothingly.

"Hmmp!" the other sniffed. "I've been wondering just what happened between her and Allen, Blair. Something did, that's sure, down in the laboratory the day after your date with him—or your first date with him. Don't look so severe, honey, your only date with him then. Joe Hart— you know, the new orderly who has a way of popping up in the most unexpected spots—told me that they had a big row and each one threatened the other. He didn't hear what it was all about, but Ridley warned Allen to watch his step and threatened to tell her grandfather something. On the other hand, Allen warned Ridley to keep her hands off someone, he didn't say who, and that if she didn't he would personally have her kicked out of the hospital. Darn it, Blair, when people play eavesdropper why on earth don't they get things straight and complete in detail? As it is we have been wondering what it was all about."

"We, Bailey?" Alex asked. "Who may 'we' be?"

"Oh, the staff in general. You know how stories get around, and Hart loves an audience and he hates Ridley. Who doesn't?"

"Hate is an ugly thing, Bailey," Alex told her soberly. "It hurts the hater worse than it does the victim."

"Maybe it does," the other answered, "but somehow no other word describes the feeling most of us here at Haddon have for Ridley. And if you don't hate her you should."

"Well," Alex replied, "I don't like her, but I don't wish her any harm. No, I don't believe I hate her exactly, Bailey. After all, she is her own worst enemy. We can safely leave her to her own future. I am not in the least worried about her." And she wondered as she spoke so smugly if she told the entire truth.

"All I can say then is that you'd better be," Bailey told her as she prepared to leave the room. "She's got it in for you and will stop at nothing. Watch your step,

Blair. I could almost wish you would leave the hospital—go into private or over to Saint Luke's or General—until she gets out, anyway."

Alex laughed. "Don't be silly, Bailey. I'm not afraid of Miss Ridley, and certainly shall not let her drive me out of here."

"Well," Bailey pointed out, "she has managed to lose you your job as supervisor. It's the first step, Blair, and I'm afraid." The older nurse's face was concerned, and Alex felt a tiny shiver of apprehension as she left the room.

What nonsense people talk, she said to herself, trying to get back her self-confidence. Ellen Ridley wouldn't dare actually attempt to injure her. After all, they were both modern women and in the same profession. She would think no more about it. But it wasn't so easily shoved aside.

Doctor Allen was in the lower hall of the nurses' section when she came downstairs some time later. He looked angry, and Alex wondered why. She had not long to wait, however, for he drew her aside and waited until they were alone before he said anything. Alex thought the world was certainly going mad. Everything seemed to be awry, and she wished she knew the answer.

"So you got fired from your job," Doctor Allen said sourly. "And I suppose you took it without a word, like the lady you are. Gosh! Alex," he exclaimed indignantly, "sometimes you make me sick!"

Alex stared at him in bewilderment. "What—what—"

"I mean it," the young man went on giving her a little shake of exasperation. "Just why did you let Halliday pay fast and loose with you like that? First she railroads you into the job, and then she dumps you out of it willy-nilly. Did she condescend to give you a reason, Alex?"

"Of course," the girl said coolly. What right had this man to talk to her like this? How dared he? "Ann Mordock is returning to the hospital and will, of course, be reinstated as night supervisor—her old position." She spoke stiffly.

"Did she tell you that?" he wanted to know, relaxing somewhat.

Alex nodded. "I—I think that is what she said. Why?"

"She will have a fight on her hands if she does," the young man told her. "Ridley wants Mrs. Anderson for the position and has been playing politics for some time to

100

bring it about. If you would have fought for your rights to the job, Alex, I doubt if she could have succeeded in her little plan. Why didn't you?"

"Because I never wanted the job in the first place," she told him emphatically. "I'm a general duty nurse, and I want nothing else. I love plain bedside nursing, Doctor, and Miss Halliday knows it because I told her. Then, too, Ann Mordock liked her job as supervisor and was excellent in that capacity and has a right to it. Miss Halliday told me she was to have it when she came back day after tomorrow—or was it tomorrow—yes, because this is to be my last night as night supervisor. That is all I know. I fail to see what Miss Ridley has to do with it."

"You wouldn't see," Doctor Allen said morosely, "because you refuse to see evil in anyone. But take it from me, Alex, you haven't heard the last of this. Not by a long shot. Why don't you insist on day work for a change? And don't let them railroad you into contagion or maternity."

Alex drew away and laughed at his concern. "Are you trying to tell me that Miss Ridley has the authority to make and alter assignments and run Haddon to suit her fancy, Doctor Allen?"

"I don't know," he replied worriedly, "I don't honestly know, but something mighty queer is going on here and I intend finding out what it is and before I get through someone is going to get her feelings hurt." He patted her nearest shoulder. "Chin up, Alex, and don't let anyone shove you around. Understand? And remember, darling, I'm always here back of you and watching day and night." He turned on his heel and hurried away, leaving Alex more confused and bewildered than ever. He had called her 'darling.' She bit her lips. Oh, well, it didn't mean a thing these days, everyone called everyone else darling. But just the same, she wished he wouldn't unless—

In the basement dining room an air of suppressed excitement seemed a tangible thing. Alex found her place and began her dinner with a feeling that she was being surreptitiously watched by the nurses at the long table with her. Bailey called to her from across the room, and one or two of the other nurses waved a greeting. The night superintendent at the head of the table—a place she had taken when she discovered she was to eat with the staff

101

and not with the hospital superintendent—paid little or no attention to what went on around her. The dinner was excellent, and the girls were hungry and for the most part were silent during the serving of the main course, but with dessert conversation picked up.

"So Ann Mordock is coming back," someone said, her voice clear and purposely distinct. "It will be good to have her back with us again. How about it, Blair? Is your nose out of joint by any chance?" It was said jokingly, and Alex replied simply, "Oh, no. Ann and I are much too fond of each other for rivalry, Cooper. I am only too glad to turn my job over to her. I'm sure she was much better as a supervisor than I ever could be. No, girls, I'm just a general duty nurse like most of the rest of you after tonight. And am I glad to be relieved!" She didn't glance in the night superintendent's direction, but was aware that she had stopped eating and was staring at her, whether in dismay or satisfaction she didn't know.

"Hear, hear!" applauded several of the nurses, and somehow Alex had the conviction that they liked her much better for her declaration. The feeling of restraint existing so long seemed to have vanished and one after another took up the subject with enthusiasm.

"Why don't you come over to pediatrics, Blair?" someone wanted to know. "You'd love the kids, and believe me we could use you. I think I'll put a bug in Halliday's bonnet to that effect."

"Gosh! Blair, we could use you in the south wing. Take it from me, our night supervisor could use help. How about it, Wimble? Am I speaking for you or am I speaking for you? Anyway, we're crowded to the doors. Come on in with us, Blair—the south wing calls."

"Just where are you going?" someone else asked.

Alex shook her head. "I haven't the least idea," she replied serenely. "It doesn't really matter so long as I get general duty nursing."

Ellen Ridley flung down her napkin and left the table leaving a vast and prolonged silence. Suddenly everyone began to clap softly and it was taken up by the entire group while Alex finished her dinner and smilingly rose to her feet. Somehow she felt as if a load had been lifted from her spirits. For the first time in her entire existence as a nurse in Haddon Memorial, she felt herself one of the staff. She went happily to her last night as supervisor in the west wing. Bailey caught up with her as she entered the elevator.

"What hit her nibs that she hustled away from the table without finishing her pie, Blair?"

"Didn't she finish it?" Blair asked. "I didn't notice."

"You wouldn't," the other retorted. "I was watching her and wondering if she could feel the animosity of the others, but not that lady. She's too thick skinned, too conceited and sure of herself. But something you said— it must have been that—touched her one vulnerable spot and she couldn't take it. I bet she's mad that you aren't heartbroken at losing your job. Well, I am if you're not, for I have a notion you may not be working in the west wing any longer."

"Well, don't forget me, Bailey," Alex told her. "I couldn't bear that. I am very fond of you, my dear, and I hope you will drop into my room whenever you find the time."

There were tears in Bailey's mild blue eyes as they parted at the third floor. Alex stood for a moment surveying the length of the third floor, and a feeling of nostalgia flooded her heart. She hadn't thought she loved the work of supervisor so much. Why, it was wonderful, and she would miss the change and variety of walking the three floors as she had been doing all these weeks. Bronson came toward her from the end room. Her face was grim, and she shook her head when she saw Alex.

"I heard the bad news, Blair," she said quietly, "and you don't have to tell me whom we have to thank for it. But never mind, honey, she isn't dead yet and she'll get hers—and plenty. Come on over and look at 314, Blair. I think she needs cheering up. The gal has the black heeby-geebies and refuses to see a single ray of light."

Alex laughed, a lump in her throat. Of course she would probably be on floor duty in a ward or in one of the other wings, but somehow this part of the hospital seemed like home to her. She went into 314 to be greeted by the patient who had but recently come through a major operation for fibroid tumor, and refused to believe that the operation was perfectly successful and that she would be better than she had been in years.

Now she wailed, "Why couldn't I have died on the

103

operating table, Nurse? Who—oh, it's you. How are you, Miss Blair?" she asked politely.

"Fine, Mrs. Wood. And they tell me you are fine, too. I am so very glad."

"But for how long? Tell me that. I'm fifty-seven years old—too old to go through an operation like that and come through safely. Don't try to flimflam me, Miss Blair. I am quite aware that my case is hopeless, but at least you might tell me how long it will be."

"Before you are well enough to leave the hospital, Mrs. Wood?" Alex asked. "Well, probably three weeks or a month at longest. We must build you up before we let you go home. You are a lucky woman, my dear," she went on, "with a wonderfully healthy constitution. It is well that you didn't put the operation off any longer. Now everything is fine and you will be home in time to superintend the spring housecleaning."

The woman's dull eyes brightened. "The cleaning was rather neglected last fall," she said apologetically. "I was feeling altogether too miserable to care." She laughed lightly. "You'll probably think I'm crazy, Miss Blair," she went on, "but I love housecleaning—love turning things topsy-turvy all over the house. George, my husband, says it's a crazy way to do, and that it's entirely unnecessary, but I notice he loves seeing it all fresh and clean after I'm through. He drags his friends in just to show them the house and brags about Hilda, our maid, who really isn't so much without me to boss her, and Jake, the handy man I have to keep jacking up every five minutes if I want anything done." Her soft laughter filled the hospital room, and Alex laughed in sympathy.

"You're a born homemaker, Mrs. Wood," she told her. "And now you will have the strength and energy to tackle the spring cleaning with real pleasure. Don't you dare get blue and depressed again, Mrs. Wood, for this is my last night as supervisor in this wing."

"I knew it!" the woman cried excitedly. "I told George that Doctor Allen was a fool if he let you float around here unattached much longer. It *is* Doctor Allen, isn't it, Miss Blair?"

Alex's face was a study in confusion and color. "Doctor Allen has nothing to do with it, Mrs. Wood," she said stiffly. "I am going back on general duty after tonight and shall probably not see you again. But you have my best wishes, and I hope your cleaning orgy is all that you hope for it. Good night, Mrs. Wood. Pleasant dreams!"

There was a gasp from the bed and a whispered, "What have I done? Oh, I am sorry if I spoke out of turn, Miss Blair."

"Think nothing of it," the girl answered quietly, although her pulses were racing with alarming speed. "We all make mistakes." She slipped from the room and went to the floor kitchen where she drew herself a glass of cold water which she sipped slowly while her heart quieted.

"You're a fool, Alex Blair," she told herself severely as she finished her drink. "Why let a bit of harmless gossip startle you? It's just because he is single, young and good looking. Some women are never satisfied unless they are matchmaking."

CHAPTER TWELVE

DOCTOR MATHEWS seemed to wear an harassed expression most of the time these days, and Alex had an idea Ellen Ridley was the cause of it. Mrs. Abigail Messer, calling herself an efficiency expert, a tall, attractive woman of forty or so, came from Chicago—Ellen Ridley's home town—to visit at the Chief's house. And Ellen Ridley brought her over to the hospital for a tour of inspection. Before her marriage, Mrs. Messer had been a superintendent of a large municipal hospital somewhere in the Midwest, and was graciously condescending to Miss Halliday, pointing out devices and customs which she considered fostered inefficiency. She held up her hands in horror that a supervisor was expected to look after more than one floor; shook her beautifully dressed head that so many nurses of forty or beyond should be working in the expensive and exclusive west wing. She raised handsome eyebrows that anyone as young and beautiful as Ann Mordock should be considered competent to handle the three floors of the west wing even for night duty. In fact, she was by no means tactful in expressing the opinion that Haddon Memorial Hospital was badly managed, and suggested a meeting of the Board of Managers in order that they might have the benefit of her experience and consider reorganizing with her competent help.

All this reached the staff via the grapevine and caused

considerable stir. Even the nurses who had never especially liked Marie Halliday hastened to her defense when this interloper, foisted upon them by the night superintendent, dared voice her criticism.

Alex Blair, in the meantime, was back at her old job as a night nurse in the west wing, and while Mordock was jubilant and the nurses there showed their delight in retaining her as one of them, the girl felt that everything was by no means smooth or settled. She had heard something of the row between Miss Halliday and Ellen Ridley over Mordock's reinstatement, and realized that in the bitter controversy she had somehow escaped complete annihilation, but she felt sure it was not for long.

The night superintendent seemed more arrogant than ever, and Doctor Hammond, the resident, and Doctor Allen, her erstwhile admirer, plainly showed their disapproval of the Chief's granddaughter—a fact of which she seemed completely unaware. With the visiting former hospital executive, they were coldly polite, but made it quite clear that their sympathies and approval were with the present incumbent.

Things reached such a point that the spring bazaar and dance, that each year was a bright spot in the somewhat drab life of the hospital, was in danger of being canceled. In fact it was at last postponed until after the Easter holidays, much to the annoyance of Miss Ridley who was eager to have her guest present at the affair. But the superintendent, backed by the staff and Board of Managers, had her way for this time. There was still far too much sickness. The hospital was far too crowded to even think of anything as unnecessary as a bazaar.

There was some difficulty encountered in bringing about a full meeting of the Board. Several members were still in Florida, one considered it quite unnecessary, and two or three questioned the wisdom of even listening to an outsider express a lot of wild and revolutionary theories about running a hospital. They had managed Haddon Memorial successfully all these years without outside interference, and saw no reason why things should not continue as they were for many years to come. But at last, Ellen Ridley had her way, and enough members of the Board were inveigled into attending and Mrs. Akers, president of the Board, presided. She did it not at all graciously, for she was a busy woman and her time and energy were pretty well taken up with church and civic duties. But she introduced the guest speaker who talked well and at length while Marie Halliday listened quietly, her face colorless and her eyes bleak. The night superintendent who made it a point to sit beside Douglas Allen, watched the faces of the audience. Doctor Allen wore a poker face and had eyes for no one but the superintendent. He felt very sorry for her, and at last moved his chair to sit beside her.

At the close of the talk, one or two members of the Board rose to question some of Mrs. Messer's statements, and Ellen Ridley frowned nervously. At last old Andrew Cabot suggested hearing what Doctor Mathews had to say about the proposed changes, and his granddaughter became alert, her cold blue gaze fastened almost hypnotically on her grandfather. Doctor Allen bit his lips, and the resident groaned aloud. The entire staff knew or thought they knew that he was putty in Ellen Ridley's hands. The Chief of Staff rose to his feet. His eyes met those of his granddaughter quietly and he spoke slowly.

"I wish to make a motion that we thank our guest speaker, Mrs. Messer, for her interesting and enlightening talk. I never knew there were so many angles to running a hospital—the primary duty of which is the care and healing of the sick. We at Haddon have no doubt been running things in a simple old-fashioned manner in that we have always made the welfare and healing of the sick our main object. Everything else has been subordinated to that. Our nurses are expected to make the care of the patient paramount. The shortage of nurses makes it necessary to increase the working hours above the legalized eight, but our girls and women show no inclination to complain. Our superintendent, Miss Halliday, has the interest of the staff at heart, and it is largely due to her efficient management that Haddon has operated smoothly and effectively for the last more than a score of trying and war broken years. Haddon is a small hospital, as such things go, and we live in a small town—only fifty thousand people live in Haddon. But this hospital is known and honored throughout the state, and we are justly proud of it. So, with the approval of the Board of Managers and the members of the staff here present I wish to move that we thank our guest

107

speaker and," he paused and cleared his throat, excused himself, and went on, "and that we continue functioning as we have been doing in the past and since the founding of Haddon Memorial almost a century ago. I thank you." He sat down amid vociferous applause.

Douglas Allen enthusiastically shook hands with Marie Halliday, who found herself unable to speak. Others present did likewise and although the president of the Board was a busy woman, she took the time to suggest a vote of thanks and of confidence be extended to the superintendent of Haddon Memorial. And it was during this demonstration which somehow waxed into thoroughly noisy acclaim that Ellen Ridley succeeded in spiriting her guest, Mrs. Messer, from the room and from the hospital. If they were missed, no one mentioned the fact.

This was Ellen Ridley's major defeat, and she surprised everyone at the way she accepted it—Doctor Allen most of all. It was later that same afternoon that the two met in the lower hall just outside the Chief's private office.

The girl laid a hand on the young surgeon's arm and said quietly, "I want to apologize for my behavior, Doug. I don't know what got into me. I hope you will forgive me and that in spite of everything we can still be friends."

Douglas Allen was embarrassed. He managed a gruff acceptance, and drew away from her detaining fingers. But the young woman held out her hand to him. "Will you shake hands on it, Doug?" she asked. And the young man took the proffered hand and gave it a limp shake. It was so that Alex Blair saw them as she came into the hall from the vestibule. She had been for a long walk along the country road adjoining the hospital grounds. Spring wasn't far away, and there were evidences of its approach all along the quiet countryside. Farmers plowing, trees showing faintly green against the vivid blue of the sky, crocuses making splotches of color in dooryards, and the occasional throaty song of a robin. Dandelions were everywhere, and somehow Alex's heart, that for the past few days had been troubled, soared. Spring was near, once again the renewal of life, the long winter of doubt and fear was over —spring and the resurrection were at hand! Her step was quick and her heart light as she came into the foyer of the hospital. The smile remained on her lips as she passed Doctor Allen and the night superintendent, and her head was high as she stepped into the elevator a few minutes later. She knew that Doctor Allen hurried along the hall after her, but she pressed the electric button and let the elevator move upward. She didn't see the smile of satisfaction on Ellen Ridley's face, nor hear the imprecation of dismay as Doctor Allen took to the stairs two at a time.

But Alex had no desire to see Douglas Allen just then, and quickly left the lift at the third floor and sped through the passage that connected the hospital with the nurses' section, being careful to close the connecting door quietly. Once inside her room, however, there was no longer a smile on her face. Suddenly the joy of a few minutes before evaporated and a feeling of depression and bleakness took its place. She slipped out of her street clothes and into a warm dressing gown. It was so that Ann Mordock found her some time later.

"What's the matter, Alex?" she asked, sitting down beside her on the broad window seat. "Don't you feel well?"

"I'm all right," the girl answered. "Just the doldrums, I guess."

"This will get you out of them then," Ann told her ecstatically. "The efficiency expert has departed as of now. Halliday, with all her faults and foibles, stays with us and everything will go on as B.M.—before Messer."

"Somehow I'm not at all surprised," Alex said without enthusiasm. "Efficiency experts never interested me much. Grandfather used to call them racketeers, and I'm enough like him to hold them in small favor."

"That isn't all my news, Alex," Ann went on, though somewhat deflated. "Ellen Ridley has accepted or is about to accept—at her grandfather's suggestion I'm sure—a position as head nurse or superintendent in a hospital somewhere in one of the western states, or maybe it's in the Philippines—I'm not sure where it is. Anyway it's somewhere miles away from Haddon. She didn't want to go, but I understand the Chief told her she had outstayed her welcome at Haddon and advised her accepting it. How's that for news, Alex?" she went on, watching her friend's sober face. "Not thrilled at that either? Well, then. Who is Bruce? He seems the alternative. The Chief advised his granddaughter 'better take Bruce.' "

Alex shook her head. "Don't mind me, Ann," she

advised. "I told you I'm in the doldrums. And I don't know any Bruce. Never heard of him."

"Then listen to this one. Doctor Allen has a chance to take over a big practice somewhere near Albany. One of the state's outstanding medicos is retiring, and going south for his or his wife's health. The Chief's fit to be tied, but Hammond thinks Allen will be a fool if he doesn't take it. There! Does that make a dent in your doldrums, honey?"

"When was all this taking place, Ann?" Alex asked. "And how do you know so much about it, anyway?"

Ann Mordock laughed. "I thought that would rouse you, Alex. Oh, he's just waiting to unburden himself to you, but you always run out on him. Just why do you treat him like poison, Alex? The guy likes you. And he really is a very fine young man."

"And you can say that after the trouble he made for you, Ann Mordock!" Alex marveled. "You have a more forgiving spirit than I have. Why, even I have been carrying a chip on my shoulder because of his losing your job for you. What happened? What alchemy has been at work to change you? I don't understand it at all."

"You will, my dear," the other said cryptically. "You will. Now suppose you get dressed, and let's get down to dinner early tonight. I'm hungry. And we are having stuffed rolled roast of veal with the first asparagus of the season."

"Honestly, Ann," Alex exclaimed feeling somehow happier, "how do you happen to know the inner workings of things as you do? I almost never do. Oh, I know that on Fridays we usually have fish for dinner. But as for the rest of the week, the meals always come as a surprise—and sometimes not a pleasant surprise either. Tell me your secret, Ann."

"Nothing to it," Ann answered nonchalantly. "I simply ask Mrs. Trimble, the housekeeper. That is, when I'm interested, I mean. Sometimes I just don't care, but I guess I'm so glad to be back that my appetite has improved. You look better, Alex. But maybe you should have Hammond give you a physical. Maybe it's spring fever."

"Oh, it's nothing serious," Alex assured her. "Just the end of a hard winter." She laughed as she fastened her uniform belt and picked up her cap. "Bruce?" she mused.

"That's the second time I've heard him mentioned in connection with Ridley. I wonder who he is."

"Probably an old beau of hers," Ann opined. "She's the type to attract men—that is some men. That Mrs. Messer and she were talking right behind me one evening—talking, quite frankly, as if I was either deaf or absent. The efficiency expert urged Ridley to quit, 'this play-acting at being a career woman. Come home and marry Bruce and take your proper place in the community.' End of quote. Evidently this Bruce has political aspirations, and Mrs. Messer emphasized the fact that he needed a wife. I didn't try to listen, Alex," she explained mirthfully. "Truly I didn't, but I was really interested. I took it that it was a question of careers—Ellen Ridley's or that of Bruce."

"Couldn't they agree on careers for both?" Alex asked.

"It seems not, from what I gathered from the conversation. But if you ask me, she'd better take Bruce and forget she ever thought of making a career of nursing, for the gal lacks about everything a good nurse requires except book learning. I understand she ranks high in that."

They left the room together and walked down the stairs arm in arm. It was good to have Ann back. Alex had missed her woefully. They were among the first to reach the basement dining room, although it was only a matter of minutes before nurses arrived in two's and three's soon filling the several long tables. Alex thought as she looked over the sea of white caps that one wouldn't suppose there was such a nurse shortage here at Haddon, but she realized how many nurses were necessary for even a relatively small hospital such as this was. The meal was good, the veal tender and well done, the stuffing savory, and the potatoes brown and crisp outside and with creamy interiors. Dinners like this were not too common at Haddon, and on these occasions the girls ate heartily amid oh's and ah's of enjoyment.

There was a full hour after dinner before they went on duty, and Ann and Alex decided to slip out for a brisk walk.

"I ate too much," Alex complained, "and I need the exercise. Our capes will be enough, and we won't need anything on our heads." She removed her cap and carried it in her hand. It was one of the rules of the hospital that no nurse should appear on the street wearing her cap. So, remembering that, both girls went out into the deceptively mild spring evening bareheaded and not too warmly clad.

"Are you two inviting pneumonia by any chance?" a jeering voice demanded behind them, and Ellen Ridley fell into step. "I can't say that I altogether blame you after that perfectly huge meal served us tonight. One would think we were a gang of stevedores or even ditch diggers, but I suppose because Haddon Memorial has been serving such meals since it was founded a hundred years ago without anyone getting an apoplexy, it will continue the bucolic practice. Bah! This place makes me sick! Stodgy, stick-in-the-mud, passé, refusing to advance. I shall be glad to go where people are at least alive." Her tone was bitter, and neither of her companions had anything to say. At the end of the hospital grounds, Alex paused for a moment.

"I think I shall go back," she said tentatively.

"Of course, go on back," Ellen Ridley snapped. "I'm not a fit companion for anyone as righteous as you two. Run along and leave me to my evil thoughts." She stalked off, and the two girls watched her hurry down the long hill and disappear into the drugstore. It wasn't until then that they turned and started to retrace their steps.

"I feel sort of sorry for her, Ann," Alex said after a moment. "She is capable and has possibilities for good. It's a shame that she doesn't use her talents to better advantage. I suppose that is what comes of being spoiled as a child. I wish I could help her. I honestly do."

"Maybe that will be the job—the life-job for Bruce, heaven help him!" Ann said. "But you keep your hands off, Alex. Ellen Ridley never forgets a fancied wrong or slight, and remember—" she paused and bit her lip.

"Remember what?" Alex asked. "What must I remember?"

"Oh, nothing, only—well, doesn't the Bible say somewhere that jealousy is cruel as the grave? Seems to me it does."

"But why should she be jealous of me, Ann? I'm sure she has no cause for it."

"Perhaps not, but she evidently thinks she has," Ann said, "which amounts to the same thing. Now don't be an idiot, Alex. Save your sympathy for someone like Berta

Miller in 419. Poor girl, and yet she may pull through all right. The Chief is going to operate in the morning, and I sort of dread tonight. It's the waiting that's so hard in these cases. Try to arrange your time so you can spend part of it with her if possible, Alex. You have been blessed with the art of soothing troubled souls and quieting jittery nerves." She laughed affectionately. "Better than a sedative, darling. Much better than anything I could suggest or Hammond could order. It's a rare gift, Alex, and I am glad you are staying on in the west wing."

"Am I staying?" Alex asked. "I didn't know. I some-how felt that in the excitement I had been lost sight of, and that when things got back to normal again I should be shifted to heaven knows where. I am relieved to know I'm staying on with you, Ann. I like it there."

They entered the brightly lighted hospital in the wake of an influx of evening visitors, and slipped into a vacant room to don caps and hang up their capes. The walk had done both girls good and they went on duty with their usual eagerness. After the anxiety and turmoil of the past weeks it was good to have things back to something like normal again. The entire west wing, indeed the whole of Haddon Memorial Hospital appeared to react as to a shot in the arm. Alex didn't know whether it was the knowledge that the night superintendent was on her way out, or merely the effect of knowing there was to be no efficiency expert nosing about interfering with the staff and making them nervous and self-conscious. Anyway, the old building seemed to glow with kindliness, and even the visitors felt it. Haddon Memorial was dear to the hearts of most of the townspeople.

CHAPTER THIRTEEN

RYKER'S DRUGSTORE, at the foot of the long hill upon which Haddon Memorial stood, was crowded at this time of the afternoon. Not all were customers, however. The high school crowd found it a good place in which to meet before starting their afternoon hikes. Of course they almost always bought cokes, and occasionally a magazine or a box of powder, but for the most part they milled about greeting their pals and being greeted in turn by them. There was something stimulating in the air of Rykers, and Alex always enjoyed going there. This late March afternoon she stopped for a tube of toothpaste and a bottle of her favorite lotion. Joey, the young drug clerk, grinned at her over the heads of a group of adolescents, and motioned them to make room for her. Alex made her wants known and stood for a moment looking about at the eager, colorful company.

"Here you are, Miss Blair," Joey said, holding out the package. "Windy today, isn't it?"

"But nice," Alex said paying for her purchases. "Spring is coming right down the hill. One can almost see it."

"Show it to me, Alex," a new voice broke in, and Alex raised her eyes to those of the tall young man who had just entered. "I feel like taking a glance at spring after what I've been through lately."

Alex smiled. "It is there for all who have eyes to see, Doctor Allen," she told him. She took a step toward the door. It seemed oddly quiet suddenly, and she felt the eyes of a score of youngsters upon her.

"Sit down for a minute and have a coke, or coffee, or even tea with me, Alex," the young man invited. "There are things I would like to discuss with you."

"The last booth is empty, Doc," Joey announced helpfully. "Say, you kids, what's become of your manners? Why don't you get out of here for a change? You take up too much room. Customers can't get any attention. Scram!" He grinned widely at the entire room, and the boys and girls laughingly took the hint and soon the store was empty except for those in the booths.

"Thanks, pal," Doctor Allen whispered, and Joey shook his own hands in acknowledgment of the appreciation.

"What will it be, Alex, coffee, tea, or a coke?" Doctor Allen asked.

"Tea, I think," Alex answered. "My English ancestry, I suppose," she smiled.

"How are things going, now that you are no longer a supervisor, Alex?" he wanted to know.

"All right so far," she replied. "I understand that I am to stay on in the west wing for a time at least."

"Good. Or as good as it could be under the circumstances," he told her. "I'm not at all pleased with the change." He added cream and sugar to his coffee, tasted it and sat back, his admiring gaze on the girl across the table. "Did you know that Jim Everts has fallen pretty hard for Ann Mordock, Alex?" he asked after a long moment, and watched her narrowly as he imparted the bit of news.

"Oh, I hoped he would, Douglas!" Alex said with enthusiasm. "Ann hasn't said anything to me but—yes, she seems different, somehow. Wait until I see her."

"And you don't mind, Alex?" the young man murmured.

"Mind?" Alex exclaimed. "Why I fixed it all up—made the date for them to meet. Oh, Douglas, I'm so happy about it! Ann is such a grand girl, and Jim's a perfect peach!"

Doctor Allen sighed. It was a long sigh, and Alex looked at him a puzzled expression on her flushed face. "What's the matter? Don't you like the idea?"

"Oh, it's quite wonderful I suppose," he muttered. "I wonder what Ellen Ridley will say when she hears about it. You know she was very much interested in Jim Everts. He seemed to admire her, too, at one time."

Alex said nothing for a moment, recalling Doctor Everts' statement that he considered Ellen Ridley a dangerous woman, and for her to beware of her. "But that was before he had met Ann," she explained. "Do you believe in love at first sight, Doctor Allen?" she asked, and immediately regretted the question.

"Yes, I suppose I do, if you mean attraction at first sight. I suppose actual love comes later with greater knowledge of each other. So you think they fell in love on that first date, Alex?" he asked interestedly.

"I don't know about Ann. But I feel sure Jim was instantly attracted to her."

"Well, Jim Everts is a fine chap, and she is a lucky girl. Both are lucky, I suppose, to have found each other, if that's the way it is."

"But I must say you don't seem too pleased about it, Doctor," Alex pouted. "Is it Ann you don't like?"

"Of course I like her. I was thinking of Ellen Ridley."

"And may I ask what Miss Ridley has to do with it?" Alex asked stiffly.

"She's going to be sore and will take it out on Mordock or you, or maybe even me. She's a strange creature, Alex," he went on.

"Who is Bruce?" Alex asked, and wondered why his name should come suddenly to her mind.

"Bruce? Bruce who?" Doctor Allen asked. "Is he someone in the hospital?"

Alex shook her head. "I think he's the man Miss Ridley's engaged to, or about to be engaged to. I don't know. But he seems very important. Don't you know anything about him?"

"Never heard of him before. Are you sure, Alex—sure of your facts, I mean?" he said, his manner showing excitement. "I hope to heaven you're right. I think I can stand things if what you say is true. Honestly, Alex, that woman is driving me insane!"

"Don't tell me she is actually pursuing you, Doctor Allen," she chided.

"Of course *not* in the way your tone implies," he answered shortly. "It's simply that she gets in my hair, and now that Jim Everts is completely out of her clutches, she may concentrate on me entirely. Does that sound caddish, Alex? I can't help it if it does. The woman's a pest and if I knew where to get hold of this Bruce I'd send him here flying. The dame bothers me. She hates me, I'm certain of that, and yet she is constantly asking my advice, demanding my assistance, consulting me about the simplest, most ordinary diagnoses. She maneuvers, if you know what I mean. And yet with it all she hates me. You don't know the half of it, Alex." He sighed and gulped the rest of his coffee.

"Poor popular young man!" Alex jeered.

Douglas Allen flushed. "You're disgusted, aren't you?" he charged.

"Not at all," Alex said demurely.

"Don't lie to me!" he hissed angrily. "You think I'm a cad, conceited, and a sissy—why don't you say so?"

"Because I don't believe you are any of those things, Doctor Allen," she said coldly, gathering up her gloves and purse. "Thank you for the tea. I think I needed it."

"You're entirely welcome, Miss Blair," Doctor Allen replied stiffly. "Are you going right back to the hospital?"

"Yes."

"I'll go with you if I may—if you're not afraid someone will report you to Halliday."

Alex gasped. "I forgot all about the rules," she told

him. "Perhaps I had better go alone. I—we might both get a reprimand." She raised laughing eyes to the young man's face. "I'm afraid those few weeks as a supervisor spoiled me, Doctor Allen."

"Oh, run along, coward!" he jeered. "I'll follow at a respectable distance."

At the door of the drugstore, Alex paused. "On second thought I believe I won't go on ahead, Douglas," she told him, her lips set in stubborn lines. "This wasn't a date, this meeting here. It was an accident and I shall treat it as such. I have broken no rules and shall not act as if I had."

"Good girl!" Douglas Allen applauded, catching her hand in his and swinging it as they started up the long hill to Haddon Memorial. Alex didn't draw it away, although she realized this hand in hand attitude might cause comment. Somehow she felt reckless, and the two climbed the hill in animated conversation.

A jeering laugh made Alex withdraw her hand and flush guiltily. There was no other sound, and the two looked around expecting to see Ellen Ridley somewhere in the neighborhood, but there was no one in sight.

"A guilty conscience," Alex said ruefully.

"Someone playing a joke on us," Doctor Allen muttered. "I wonder what would happen if we walked right into the hospital hand in hand or even arm in arm. Do you suppose I have compromised you, Alex?" he went on, smiling into her rueful face. "If so, I stand ready and willing to make an honest woman of you."

"Don't even joke about such things, Doctor Allen," the girl snapped. "I have done nothing reprehensible. Ann and I often walk hand in hand or arm in arm. I refuse to feel guilty."

Douglas Allen threw back his head and laughed gleefully. "How serious you are, Alex," he chided. "And I don't think I feel exactly flattered that you class me in the same category as your friend Ann. After all, my dear, I'm a man, you know."

They were drawing near to the hospital and Alex glanced about. Where had that jeering laugh come from? The Chief's house showed no signs of life. Except for a few late visitors, most of them on their way out, the hospital and grounds looked deserted. Strange.

"Don't worry your head about anyone reporting you to

117

Halliday, Alex," Doctor Allen assured her. "I'm going to stop in there right now and mention the fact of our chance meeting and subsequent stroll up Bradley Hill." His voice was slightly derisive, and Alex bridled, feeling his unspoken disapproval of her childish fear of a reprimand.

"Don't bother," she snapped. "Let it ride. It isn't at all likely that anyone is enough interested in my actions to report them. Thank you for the tea, Doctor Allen, and good-bye!" She spoke with finality. She was hurt and angry. What right had he to criticize her? It was he who had placed her in this position, and he had no right to disapprove of her desire to obey the hospital rules.

Doctor Allen opened the heavy door and stood aside for her to enter, which she did with head high and shoulders back. It was unfortunate that Ellen Ridley should be coming along the hall toward the exit. She bowed coolly and unsmiling at Alex and went on out. What had become of Doctor Allen? Alex wanted desperately to turn her head and find out, but she didn't have to as he suddenly appeared before her, nonchalantly removing his gloves. She stopped and frankly stared.

"How—where—?" she stammered, wide-eyed.

"I still have your welfare at heart, my dear," he told her reassuringly.

Alex gasped. "Forget my welfare," she snapped.

"Impossible," he told her, and went on into the Chief's office.

Alex was annoyed to find that she was trembling— whether from anger or dismay she didn't know. Who was it laughed there on the hill? It certainly sounded like Ellen Ridley, but it couldn't have been because she was in the hospital. She met her there in the hall. And how on earth was it possible for Douglas Allen, who had stood on the doorstep behind her just a moment before, to come strolling down the hall toward her now? It was all very puzzling and Alex's head whirled. She walked to the elevator, but before she could press the button, Doctor Allen joined her.

"Don't let my agility bother you unduly, Alex," he told her soothingly. "I simply sprinted around to the side door when I caught a glimpse of Ridley on her way out. Nothing to it. It just required a fast bit of foot work. Don't be mad at me, Alex." He pressed the elevator button and jumped out as the door started to close and the lift began its climb upward. "That was a crow or a loon who laughed, darling."

Alex was smiling as she entered her room a few minutes later. Ann Mordock was waiting for her.

"Did you have a nice walk, Alex?" she asked as Alex removed her coat and hung it in her closet. "Meet anyone you know?"

Alex swung around. "How did you know?" she demanded.

"Know what?" Ann asked, frowning at the other's tone.

"That Doctor Allen came into the drugstore while I was there, and we had tea together—or rather, I had tea and he had coffee. I simply forgot that I am no longer a supervisor, Ann, and so have not the privileges I had when I was."

Ann laughed. "You surely are not letting a little thing like that spoil the memory of what was probably a pleasant encounter, are you?" she chided.

"It wasn't especially pleasant," Alex answered. "He's scared to death of Ridley, Ann. Can you imagine anything so silly?"

"Oh, I don't know," Ann replied. "Better and stronger men than Douglas Allen have been compromised before this, and no doubt will be again as long as there are predatory females and a man shortage." She was laughing as she talked, but Alex felt there was no real mirth in her laughter, and she stiffened.

"I fail to see anything to laugh at, Ann," she told her friend. "It is just plain silly to me. I have always believed and still do, that no man has to date a girl, much less marry her, if he doesn't want to. Hmmp!" she scoffed. "The stronger sex, indeed! What's strong about it?"

"I have a hunch," her friend said seriously, "that Ellen Ridley is out to marry Douglas Allen and soon, too. That may sound fantastic, Alex," she went on, "but something I heard this afternoon when I was in the library downstairs made me realize how really determined the woman is."

Alex stared. "Just what did you hear, Ann, and was it eavesdropping or were you in on the conversation?"

Ann's face wore a guilty expression. "I had a perfect right to be there, Alex," she said defiantly. "I was already there when the Chief came in and we talked for awhile, and then Ridley entered and I slipped into the alcove and sat down out of the way. I don't know if she knew I was there or not. Surely the Chief knew. He must have known. Anyway, he asked her what she had heard lately from Bruce. Bruce again. He spoke almost jocularly, and she snapped at him. 'Nothing!' she answered. 'And I haven't changed my original plans yet.' And when her grandfather told her not to be a. fool, that his assistant was already interested in someone else or words to that effect, she flew into a rage and told him she would marry Douglas Allen or see that he never married anyone else. It was a threat and she meant it. The Chief tried to reason with her. Told her she was unwomanly, out of her mind, and quite unsuitable to be Doctor Allen's wife, but she wouldn't listen. She finally told him to mind his own business and let her manage her life as she saw fit. Honestly, Alex, it was very dramatic but terribly unlovely, if I can use that term. I wonder if Ridley. is well balanced. I have never heard anything more insane than her ranting. She declared that even if she hated Allen she intended marrying him just the same. Can you imagine such talk? She went out at last, and I heard the poor old Chief muttering to himself. I was afraid to show myself and at last he went out, too, and I simply crept away feeling almost like a criminal." She laughed ruefully.

"It seems incredible," Alex whispered, her face pale and her gray eyes dark with horror. "What did she mean— that he should never marry anyone else, Ann? Do you think she intends killing him?"

Ann shook her head. "Probably nothing as drastic as that, Alex," she answered. "No doubt she meant that she could spoil his chances of marrying anyone else, maybe through gossip or something of that nature."

"I don't like it, Ann," Alex murmured. "Why doesn't her grandfather do something? Why doesn't he send for this Bruce whoever he is? Maybe if she saw him unexpectedly she might forget her desire for Doctor Allen."

"Don't worry about it, Alex," Ann told her. "Perhaps I should not have repeated what I heard, but it was just to prove to you that sometimes a man can't help himself. But she hasn't married him yet, and maybe he can fool her —beat her to it, and marry the girl the Chief hinted that he was interested in. I wonder who she can be? One of our Haddon nurses do you suppose, Alex, or could it be a town girl? I heard he is invited everywhere. Jim Everts told me he is very popular. There are some very pretty girls here in Haddon—among them my own cousin, Phyllis. You have met her, haven't you?"

"Yes, I have met your cousin," Alex answered apathetically. "Is she after him, too, Ann?" she asked.

Ann shook her head. "I don't think so, although she thinks he is quite wonderful. She spoke of a Carol Foster— her father is president of the Forge and Tool Plant here in Haddon. Rich as all get out. It seem the Fosters think highly of Doctor Allen, and he is often their guest on various occasions. It might be a good thing for him to be connected with a family like that. I understand he hasn't a sou." ,

"I'm sure I wouldn't know," Alex replied shortly.

"Oh, well, he doesn't really need money—a man like Doctor Allen. He's clever and should be able to make his way in the world without it. Unless, of course, Ridley gets her hooks into him."

"I never heard you talk like this before, Ann," Alex said, puzzled at her friend's determination to stick to the subject. "You aren't given to gossip, and it isn't at all like you. Just what is your object now?"

"Oh, I just felt like doing a bit of gossiping, Alex," she answered airily. "After all, even an ice princess must relax occasionally. And I like Doctor Allen and detest Ellen Ridley. I sometimes wish I had played my cards better, and maybe he would have settled on me instead of on heavens knows who. Anyway, I assure you, I should have given Miss Ridley a run for her money. She would have given up long ago."

"It isn't too late yet, is it?" Alex asked, suddenly demure. "Or is it that your heart is already involved with someone else? It couldn't possibly be anyone I know, could it? Jim Everts, perhaps?"

Ann Mordock gasped. "Don't be ridiculous!" she cried. "Why I have only met the man once—twice anyway. What—"

"A little bird told me all about it," Alex said, "and I assure you I am very happy at the way the affair is

121

progressing. But just where does that leave me, Ann?" she asked ruefully.

"Just where you were before, my dear," her friend pointed out. "Why don't you wake up, Alex? Douglas Allen is head-over-heels in love with you, and you treat him like something no self-respecting cat would drag in. No wonder Ridley thinks she can have her own way, and take him right from under your nose without your moving a muscle to stop her. As the football coach tells his players, 'Get in there and fight, fight, fight!' "

Alex laughed at the other's vehemence. "Now it's you who are being ridiculous, Ann Mordock," she said ruefully. "Maybe Jim Everts knows more than I do about it, but I assure you Doctor Allen has never given me any reason for thinking he is in love with me, except—"

"Except?" Ann pounced upon the word. "Except what?"

"Nothing," Alex answered. "And if you are ready let's go down to dinner. I feel that I need food after all this wild discussion."

They moved on down the stairs and into the basement dining room. The place at the head of the table was vacant, and Alex wondered where the night superintendent was. She had not long to wait, however, for someone two or three seats down the table from her expressed disgust that she had met Miss Ridley and the Chief's assistant in the Chief's own car and headed for town. "And," she informed her listeners acidly, "the fair Ellen appeared animated and mighty pleased with herself, but Allen, poor lug, looked as if he was bound for the guillotine." She laughed shrilly, and one of the older nurses present hushed her peremptorily. "Was there an accident somewhere near here?" the talkative nurse asked. "I haven't heard of any, but they were both in white—just plain hospital white, as if they were bound for a job of work some place."

"I bet," someone jeered, derisively. "Anything to get the handsome surgeon off to herself—poor guy. Lucky Ridley!"

"Isn't it the limit how everything seems to come her way?" someone else pointed out.

Alex felt Ann's gaze on her, but went on eating although there was no taste in the food. Just what was happening? And could a woman of Ellen Ridley's type actually

122

compromise anyone as sensible and plain good as Douglas Allen? She didn't know. She gulped the last of her coffee and rose from the table, among the first to leave. Ann caught up with her as she headed for the elevator.

"I just heard there was an accident, Alex, over on the Boulevard. An Inter-urban bus went off the road. A couple of trucks were mixed up in it someway. The ambulance with the Chief and a couple of nurses had already gone. So—well, I don't see what good Ridley will be there, but maybe I'm prejudiced."

"He could have gone in the ambulance instead of the Chief," Alex said more to herself than to Ann. "And Ridley's a night superintendent, not a nurse. After all, it isn't the Chief's place to ride in an ambulance."

"When the Chief is Ridley's grandfather it is, Alex," Ann said.

"I see, " Alex murmured.

"I hope you do," her friend told her. "And I hope you will do something about it."

It was a troubled Alex who went off duty toward morning, and her sleep was restless and unprofitable. She ate an unsatisfactory breakfast and went out alone. She had to get away from the hospital to think. She headed for the open country. She had the entire afternoon to herself, and hoped she would meet no one who would spoil her plans.

CHAPTER FOURTEEN

SEVERAL DAYS PASSED, and each time Alex saw Doctor Allen, he was accompanied by Ellen Ridley. Once Ann Mordock tried to break up the combination by inviting the night superintendent to examine the chart and foot of Roger Oakland in 316. The elderly man had been suffering from a prolonged, though considered not too serious, case of diabetes and although until now threatened with an amputation was beginning to show definite signs of improvement through the use of the Burdick's Rhythmic Constrictor for dilating the veins in the foot and forcing the blood down into the toes where the circulation was faulty.

It had been a long slow process and the patient should have been under the care of specials but, due to the continued nurse shortage, Haddon Memorial was managing without them wherever possible. Ann and the other supervisors in the west wing were proud of Mr. Oakland's improvement. Miss Ridley, however, seemed not unduly excited. She gave a cursory glance at the chart, let her gaze rest for a moment on the still inflamed and swollen foot, then turned restlessly toward the hall.

"Probably will recover without amputation, Mordock," she pronounced shortly. "Still, an increase of insulin should help."

"I have never been given insulin," the patient said sharply. "I never intend becoming an addict."

Ellen Ridley stared at him arrogantly for a long moment, then turned and left the room.

"Hmmp!" the man muttered. "And who does she think she is?"

"Haven't you ever met the night superintendent, Mr. Oakland?" Ann asked.

"If that's who she is then I never want to meet her," he answered flatly. "Insulin indeed. Not me."

Ann followed Ridley down the long corridor, but when she reached the elevator it was already mounting upward and she gave an exclamation of disgust. But maybe Doctor Allen and Alex had had a few minutes to themselves. She wondered if they made good use of it. The elevator descended and Douglas Allen stepped out. He grinned when he saw Ann.

"Thanks, pal," he said softly as he went into the first room.

"Don't mention it," Ann smiled.

It was some time later and Alex, on the fifth floor, was busy massaging tired old Mrs. Earle in 518, that Ellen Ridley walked in. She cast a quick look around the room, and went out without uttering a word. Alex smiled to herself. It was all very silly and certainly most unethical. She wondered why the Chief put up with her—even if she was his granddaughter. Why didn't he send her packing back to that mythical Bruce? Old Mrs. Earle grunted with pleasure as Alex rubbed her aching back.

"That's good, Miss Blair. Nobody rubs the aches and pains out of me like you do. What did that Ridley woman want poking her nose in here? Was she looking for someone or something?" She chuckled gleefully. "I bet she was looking for that good looking young surgeon, Allen. Too bad if she gets him. What's the matter with you, my dear? A man-hater?"

"I—I don't think so," Alex replied. "There, do you feel better now? Suppose I get you a glass of warm milk, and then you turn over and try to sleep. Are your pillows all right? Okay, Mrs. Earle. I'll get your milk."

She left the room and met Ann Mordock just outside. She, too, seemed to be looking for someone. What was this? A game of hide and seek?

"Have you seen either Ridley or Doctor Allen?" the supervisor asked as she paused for a moment.

"Miss Ridley was in 518 just a minute ago, Ann," Alex said. "I think she was looking for someone, too. Was it you, by any chance?"

"You know better than that, Alex," Ann answered. "Well, I have a message for her. If you see her, tell her the Chief wants her to come over to the house at once. He said she has an important visitor." She lowered her voice. "It could be Bruce!"

"No such luck," Alex replied. "And I'm not at all likely to see her. She doesn't care for the fifth floor for some reason. Have you looked on the fourth or even the third, Ann? She must be on one of them—or is she?" She went into the floor kitchen, got milk from the refrigerator, and heated it carefully. It must be just right or Mrs. Earle wouldn't touch it. She hummed softly to herself as she watched the kettle, and was startled when Doctor Allen came into the room.

"Has Ridley been up here tonight, Alex?" he asked, his eyes dancing with mischief. "I hear her grandfather wants her."

"She was here a moment ago, but I thought she was looking for you. Didn't she find you?"

"Mmmm!" he muttered shaking his head. "Not yet." He turned as the soft whirr of the elevator reached them, and peered into the hall. "Here she comes, Alex," he groaned.

"I'll meet her," the girl said, smothering a wild desire to laugh. It was all so very ridiculous. So impossible. This was a hospital. What on earth was the meaning of this woman hounding one of the doctors this way? She went into the hall and closed the door behind her. The latch caught. Forgotten was the milk for Mrs. Earle. Forgotten

125

was everything but the fact that this predatory female was determined to get hold of her man. She looked into the eyes of the night superintendent and asked sweetly, "Did you receive your grandfather's message, Miss Ridley?"

"I did, Blair," she answered haughtily. "And please remember that Doctor Mathews is not my grandfather while I am on duty. He is Chief of Staff. Yes, I received his message, and he can wait my convenient time for an answer. I have business with Doctor Allen."

"Oh," Alex said blandly, "then I won't detain you. Perhaps he is on the next floor—pediatrics, or maybe the small o.r."

"You are so helpful!" the woman said ironically as she walked away, then stopped abruptly as she met the derisive smile on Bailey's plain face. "And what's so funny, Bailey?" she demanded curtly. "I must say that my grandfather has been badly fooled by the class of nurses accepted in this hospital."

"Not to mention night superintendents," Bailey snapped, her eyes glaring angrily at the insult to her beloved Haddon.

"How dare you? I shall make it a point to report your impertinence, Bailey," Ridley told her vindictively. "And believe me, I shall be glad when I can leave this grossly mismanaged institution."

"You and me both," Bailey muttered, but quite loud enough for the other to hear. But the night superintendent stalked down the long dim hall, and pressed the elevator button savagely.

"You should not have antagonized her, Bailey," Alex told her, shaking her head. "Although I don't blame you. Only now there will be more trouble. Oh, my goodness! I forgot Mrs. Earle's milk." She returned to the kitchen. The milk had boiled over, and Doctor Allen was eying the scorched pan ruefully.

"I never noticed until it boiled over, and then I put out the gas," he told her. "What a smudge! Thanks for saving my life, Alex," he went on as she got down another kettle and poured in fresh milk. "Where did she go? Down or up?"

"I didn't notice," Alex said. "I was too upset. She is going to report Bailey who, she says, was impertinent. But I don't blame Bailey, Douglas. I know one thing though. If someone doesn't get that woman out of here something terrible is going to happen. I don't intend to stand much more."

"Let's elope, Alex," the young man urged, his lips close to her ear. "I haven't anything to offer you but love, honey, but I've got a heart full of that. Will you? Put me out of my misery, darling. Say yes," he whispered.

Alex's heart pounded. Her eyes on the slowly heating milk, she whispered back. "I think you're afraid of Ellen Ridley, Douglas," she told him. "You need police protection more than you do a wife, but this is neither the time nor the place for a proposal of marriage, Doctor. There, it's absolutely right this time and a good thing, too, for we have just about run out of milk."

"Oh, here you are!" a voice said coldly, and the night superintendent stared suspiciously at them from the doorway. "What is the meaning of this—this charade?" she demanded. "And what are you hanging around the kitchen for, Douglas Allen?" she asked, her blue eyes cold with fury. "Halliday shall hear of this, Blair."

"All right," Alex answered, equally furious at this woman who was making mischief for them all in this hospital. "Doctor Allen has a perfect right to be here in the kitchen with me. You tell her, Douglas. We didn't intend announcing it until we were ready to leave, but you have forced our secret from us, Miss Ridley." She slipped her hand through Doctor Allen's arm and leaned against him, her bright head pressed against his shoulder.

"Meet my wife, Ellen," he said proudly, and felt Alex's start of surprise. "So, report that bit of news to Miss Halliday, if you like. If she fires Alex, she'll have to fire me, too, and then what will the Chief have to say to that? By the way, I understand you have a guest over at the house, Ellen. Bruce is here."

"Bruce?" Ellen Ridley cried. And Alex hushed her sternly.

"Have you forgotten this is a hospital, Miss Ridley?" she asked severely.

"Oh, shut up!" Ellen Ridley sniffed disdainfully. "So you're married? I don't believe it."

"Suit yourself," Doctor Allen told her airily, his arm close about Alex. "Darling, I think Mrs. Earle has waited long enough for her milk, don't you? Run along. I have a

127

few things to look after before I can call it a day—or a night. Be seeing you. Good night, Miss Ridley. I wish you would keep our little secret for awhile longer."

"I told you I didn't believe it, Douglas Allen, and I still don't," she said sharply. "You and that—that mysterious Alex or Lisa Blair are trying to pull a fast one, but I have ways of finding out things, my friend, and I'll discover just what that girl is hiding here for if it ruins us all. Ice princess indeed!" she scoffed. "I'll say she's anything but cold, that one. A fast worker and decidedly a hot number. Mark my words, Douglas Allen, there'll come a time," she went on furiously and insanely, "when you'll rue the day you ever made an enemy of Ellen Ridley."

"Tut, tut!" the young man chided, trying hard to keep his temper from exploding. "You sound like a fish-wife or a hussy in a fourth-rate melodrama. That's no way for a nurse—a night superintendent to talk. Certainly not for a lady. Shame on you!"

She stared at him for a moment, then swept away and sent the elevator downward. And he thought it was a good thing the lift was electrically operated and controlled, or both elevator and its occupant would have certainly crashed in the basement.

An anxious frown on his face, he went in search of Ann Mordock. It was getting late and he wondered if the Chief's visitor was still waiting. He found Ann on the fourth floor, and asked for a few minutes of her time. They, too, went into the floor kitchen, and there Doctor Allen related the events that had just happened. Ann choked with suppressed laughter, but the young man's face was grave.

"Do you suppose there is anything in that threat of Ridley's, Ann?" he asked. "Can she make trouble for Alex? Has Jim told you anything about her? I won't believe there's a thing wrong, Ann. Don't make any mistake on that score. I adore Alex, and no matter what happened in the past I want her for my wife. But Ridley can be pretty devilish when she wants to be. And she usually wants to be. She's got it in that mean head of hers that Alex is hiding something—is guilty of something. Can you think of any way I can protect her?"

"You could marry her now—at once or as soon as legally possible, Douglas," Ann told him. "I think after it's all over Ridley might sort of lose interest. Anyway, she would know you couldn't marry her—if that is what she's after, and I have a hunch that is her idea, my lad. Why don't you make it real, Douglas? The marriage, I mean? It has been done before."

"But I don't like doing it that way, Ann," he demurred.

"It's the only way I can think of," the girl answered. "You love her, and somehow I have the idea that Alex loves you. Why waste time?"

"Okay," he replied. "I'll try to make Alex see my point, Ann. Perhaps if she thinks she is protecting me she will consent. But try to keep it as quiet as possible. Three days. I hope the man over at the Chief's *is* Bruce. Maybe he can keep her out of our hair. Blast the woman! I hope to heaven I never come across anyone like her again."

"By the way, Douglas," Ann asked, her eyes dancing with mischief. Somehow she couldn't seem to take any of this seriously. "Just when did this marriage take place? Make a good story if you must prevaricate. I'll back you up." She laughed gleefully. "The ice princesses are melting fast, Doctor Allen," she said. "But then, it's spring, and anything can happen in spring."

"Do you suppose we could have been married before either of us came here, Ann?" he asked. "That might be the reason why I came here at all—just to be with my estranged wife." He grinned ruefully. "Just as if I could ever become estranged from Alex, or Lisa, as I suppose I should call her now." He frowned darkly. "All this deception sickens me, Ann," he told her. "I hate a liar—" He paused at Ann's soft laughter. "I know, that was a whopper but I got excited and it seemed the only way to stop that woman. Is she human do you suppose or a vampire in female form?"

"Oh, she's merely a female in love, Doctor," Ann pointed out. "Love works that way with some people. It does strange things."

"Love!" he muttered angrily. "She hates me. You should hear her sometimes and watch her expression, it is positively fiendish. Well, I hope it all comes out right. But I'm frank to say I'm afraid for Alex."

Ann's eyes were sympathetic, but she shook her head. "I think you underestimate Alex, Doctor," she said. "Alex has an amazing amount of courage stored up in that lovely body of hers and a keen sense of values. I doubt if anyone living is able to make a fool of her or swerve her from her purpose if she knows she is right. Don't worry about Alex, my lad. If she feels that you need her—that you should be protected from Ellen Ridley—she will do anything, even to the point of sacrificing her own life, to save you. I know Alex Blair, Doctor, and I have implicit faith in her judgment. If she decides to marry you she will go through with it, and nothing and no one on earth will stop her. There, have I helped you—strengthened the old morale a bit?"

Doctor Allen grinned ruefully at the supervisor, and nodded his head. "I'm going back to fifth, Ann, and make a date for tomorrow instead of next day as we planned. The sooner this is buttoned up the better. Bless you, Ann Mordock!" he murmured giving her a quick hug. "May you and Jim have nothing like this to contend with."

He hurried from the room and raced down the dim and silent corridor to the elevator and up to the fifth floor. Alex was nowhere in sight. Bailey and Morrison stood at the desk in the alcove in whispered conversation.

"Has Blair left?" he asked.

"Just a minute ago, Doctor Allen," Bailey murmured sympathetically. "If you hurry, you may catch her before she reaches the annex. Would you like me to go after her, Doctor?"

But Doctor Allen was already on his way, and the two nurses, just now awaiting the appearance of reliefs, looked meaningly at each other.

And Alex was two-thirds through the covered passageway that connected the nurses' quarters with the main hospital when she heard running footsteps and a soft mention of her name. She stopped and looked behind her.

"Wh—what is it?" she asked startled. What else was going to happen before this crazy night ended?

"I had to see you, Alex," he said nervously. "Can we talk here?"

"Not very well," she told him. "Do you know what time it is? Twenty minutes of five. It's nearly morning, Douglas, and you have been up all night. Run along and get some sleep. Tomorrow is another day, and nothing so terribly important can possibly happen now."

"Don't fool yourself, Alex," he muttered. "I'm worried

about you. Try to be careful. And I must see you tomorrow —no, today, this afternoon and keep our date tomorrow, too, darling. I have been talking with Ann and we must make plans—foolproof plans, Darling, darling!" he murmured, catching her in his arms and holding her close. "I wish we were really married. I wish it was all true, and I should never have to leave you."

Alex rested for a brief space, her heart beating hard against his own, while their lips clung for a long, world shattering, soul satisfying moment. A door banged near at hand, and with a little cry of dismay she slipped from his arms and sped along the passage and in at the door of the annex, while Doctor Allen, his head a-whirl turned slowly and went back the way he had come.

Outside the east was brightening. Even as he looked, long streamers of crimson and gold shot up from the horizon. Mr. Sun was announcing to the world that he was about to make his appearance, but warning the waiting earth not to expect too much in the way of pleasant weather. Rain would very likely drench the countryside before evening. Wasn't it a truism, important to mariners and landlubbers alike, "red sky in the morning, sailors take warning"?

Douglas Allen paused to watch the sun's fiery approach and, in spite of the dire warning of storms to come, he somehow felt less apprehensive, stronger and much happier. Perhaps it was due to the pressure of warm young lips against his own, or the memory of a pliant, yielding body in his arms. His wife! He threw back his head and marched with militant tread to the doctor's house, mounted the stairs to his room, and fell gratefully into bed without removing his clothes.

Over in the room Alex Blair had occupied for five years there was no sound except for the faint ticking of the clock. The room was beginning to brighten from the red glare of a triumphantly rising sun. A faint smile curved the lips of the sleeping girl. It had been a hectic night—an astonishing, almost unbelievable night, the most unbelievable part of which was that unexpected meeting and embrace. She had yawned and stretched as she lay for a moment trying to quiet her wildly beating pulses. She had thought to remain awake for a long time reviewing the incredible happenings of the past hours, but she was very weary. Almost against her will her tired body relaxed, her heavy eyelids drooped, and sleep cried out to possess her. She told herself that everything would be straightened out in the morning, and at last she gave up the unequal fight and slept.

CHAPTER FIFTEEN

IT WAS NOT Bruce who waited impatiently the return of Ellen Ridley from what he supposed was rigorous duty at the hospital, but the business head of a hospital in western Illinois—one of the institutions sadly in need of a superintendent of nurses, or even an assistant superintendent. The man, a serious-minded businessman, financial manager of a small but well-equipped hospital, was determined to examine very closely any applicant from the position. The hospital in question had suffered from inefficiency before, and he was determined that this time he would meet and personally investigate the applicant before adding her to the staff.

The gentleman had met and admired Doctor Mathews and felt confident that a granddaughter of his must, as a matter of course, be competent, efficient and above reproach in every respect. So he had come East with the idea that if Ellen Ridley should be all that her connection with Doctor Mathews implied, his troubles were over and his beloved hospital was in luck.

But when midnight passed, followed by one and two o'clock, with Doctor Mathews trying hard to remain the perfect host, the visitor lost considerable of his enthusiasm for anyone, even the granddaughter of the rather famous Doctor Mathews, who could treat him in such an indifferent and disrespectful manner. So, when the tall clock in the hall of the stately old house struck three deep and sonorous notes, he rose to his feet and with the briefest of good-byes, left the room and the house. Doctor Mathews yawned wearily, and gratefully went to bed. He had hoped that if Ellen should get away from Haddon Memorial and certain members of the staff, she might come to her senses, and might even become a good superintendent of nurses, although he still had his doubts. Too bad, too, because Ellen was clever—fine mind, wonderful memory, and was quick as chained lightning. It was her disposition that was the handicap. Her unfortunate manner. He sighed, but was soon asleep.

"What did you do with Bruce, Grandfather?" his granddaughter demanded late next morning. "And what did he want?"

"Bruce?" the old man murmured. "I didn't see Bruce. Was he here, too?"

"You sent for me."

"Of course, but you didn't see fit to obey the summons. It was a gentleman from—now he told me, but it has slipped my mind. Somewhere near Chicago, I believe. He was offering you a position as superintendent of nurses, or even assistant, in a small but well equipped institution of eighty beds. But I have a notion he lost interest when you failed to show up. Anyway, he left at three this morning, and I have heard nothing from him since. What ails you, girl? Don't you know that you can't play fast and loose with a position such as that one was? Now what do you plan on doing? You can't stay here much longer. You long ago wore out your welcome. The members of the staff of Haddon Memorial don't care for you."

"Any more than I care for them," the young woman snapped. "But I assure you, I intend to stay here just as long as I want to—or until I have accomplished my purpose. So you might as well make the best of it, Grandfather. How did Bruce come into the picture?" she asked after a moment. "Who knows anything about Bruce here?"

The old man shook his head. He looked worn and old this morning, and wished devoutly that the girl's mother were on hand to manage her. What to do. He rose at last and left the house. The hospital was his haven—the only haven he could depend upon. There he was master. Chief of Staff. Honored and looked up to. He squared his shoulders and walked the short distance to the beloved building next door. And the years fell from him when he walked through the heavy front door. In his private office, Hammond, the resident, and Douglas Allen, his assistant, were in heated discussion. His step was without sound, and he heard Hammond say sourly—

"The woman is disrupting the entire nursing staff, Doug. Already two of them—Mason and Jackson, are quitting. They are both dependable nurses. Halliday talked to them. I talked to them. But they simply won't endure Ridley's highhanded methods. They are neither of them young, but they are both excellent nurses. Saint Luke's will snap them up in a hurry. I tell you Haddon Memorial can't afford to lose them. We need every nurse we have. I wish you would talk to the Chief, Doug. Maybe you can get him to use pressure."

"Doctor Allen doesn't have to tell me anything, Tom," the Chief told the house physician. "I know all about it. And there isn't a thing I can do unless I have her disqualified, which I hesitate to do, so I reckon she will stay on here until she tires of it—which I hope and pray will be soon. After all, gentlemen, she is an excellent nurse and—my granddaughter," he added somewhat ruefully. The others nodded. They understood. "By the way," the Chief went on, "did Bruce come here last evening?"

"Bruce who?" Doctor Hammond asked.

"Wasn't it Bruce with you when you sent for Ellen last night, Chief?" Doctor Allen asked. "I don't know where I got that idea, but I certainly thought that's who your caller was, and I guess I told her so."

"Wishful thinking, my boy, just wishful thinking," Doctor Mathews told him. "But at that it gives me an idea. Yes, indeed, it may work. What's on your mind this morning, Tom?" he asked the resident.

"I should like you to take a look at young Danny Capello this morning, Doctor. He seems about ready for you. Morale high, pulse steady, and blood pressure normal. He had a good night, and Watson seems to think he'll never be readier than he is right now. Which o.r., Chief?"

"It's a major. See that the main o.r. is ready, and notify Grant, Nye and Burgess to be ready in thirty minutes. Get word to Doctor Widmer, too. Maybe you should get in touch with Howland over at General, and you might send word to Saint Luke's, too. Now get out, both of you. Meet me in the main o.r. in thirty minutes, Doctor Allen."

The two doctors left the room. "I'll run over and see Danny," Doctor Allen suggested. "Does his mother know, Tom?"

"I phoned her neighbor who promised to get word to her, but I don't suppose she'll come. After all, Danny's been here for months, and she has a half-dozen or more other kids to look after. See you later, Doug."

134

"Okay," Allen answered, and slipped out into the mild spring morning. The sun was pale now and the wind damp. It looked as if the prophesy of the morning would become a fact and soon. He walked the length of the long building and entered by another door. This was the east wing housing the wards, and was newer in architecture, but to Doctor Allen's mind not nearly so attractive. The wards were crowded, and he greeted each patient with a cheery word or friendly pat on the shoulder. In the last bed, a large-eyed boy of twelve lay partially propped up reading a comic book, and grinning from ear to ear as he turned the pages. He shouted a greeting as Doctor Allen drew near, and the young surgeon paused to visit. Watson, the day supervisor joined him.

"I think this is it, Doctor," she told him, smiling at the patient. "We're all ready for the big adventure, aren't we, Danny?"

"S-sure," the boy answered. "I—I been here too long. I guess they want to kick me out, Doc," he grinned, and Doctor Allen knew he was whistling in the dark.

"That's the spirit, Danny," he said cheerily. "I'm going with you, you know. Just to see that everything's okay," he grinned.

"All the way, Doc?" the boy asked. "You goin' all the way?"

"All the way," Douglas Allen promised, and made a silent prayer that the way, though perilous, might be safe and health-giving for this plucky youngster.

At eleven o'clock the operating theater of Haddon Memorial Hospital was the scene of another of those miracles for which Doctor Mathews was famous. Surgeons and physicians from other hospitals, as well as several nurses and a few interested laymen, filled the gallery and watched with bated breath as the tall old surgeon worked swiftly and unfalteringly, so that this child of poverty should one day walk erect as others walked. It was a long operation, and when it was over and the Chief was scrubbing in the adjacent washroom, with admiring visitors pouring congratulatory words into his deaf ears, he felt strangely elated. Danny Capello would walk again! He would walk, tall and straight, like other boys! But somehow he was tired. Maybe he should give it up, and retire as Ellen urged him to do. Maybe he was too old for this sort of thing. He dried his hands, and turned to the group of admiring surgeons.

"Not bad for an old feller, was it?" he grinned.

"You should feel very proud, Doctor," one of the visiting surgeons said. "We are, for we have witnessed a fine piece of work."

"Proud?" the Chief grunted. "Me? Why I was merely the human instrument, Doctor. My hand was guided by a Greater Hand than mine. You see, Doctor, I always ask for that Hand on mine before I ever dare take up a scalpel. It's the only way, my friends. The only way."

One by one the visitors left, and if one or two of the younger men scoffed that Mathews was getting old, they were properly rebuked by the others. There was too much truth in what the old surgeon had said. For they, too, had often felt the need of that Guiding Hand.

Alex had told Douglas Allen that she had a dental appointment at two-thirty that afternoon, and he said he would wait outside the building for her. Alex demurred. It was against the rules, but the young surgeon overcame her scruples, and they met at three and drove over to a small restaurant on the outskirts of town.

"Now relax, Alex," Doctor Allen urged, as they found seats in a far corner of the room. "This had to be. We have got to decide what is best to be done. I pulled a boner, I know. But I was honestly so excited that I said the first thing that came into my head. Wishful thinking, probably, darling, but—"

"That story can't possibly be verified, Douglas," Alex said a frown on her face. "Then, too, I can't stand deception. A lie never accomplished anything worthwhile and—oh, Douglas, why did you make such a wild statement? I know, I know," she went on, "you were excited. So was I, but I'm sure Ridley didn't believe you. Now what are we going to do?"

"And you think the story won't hold water?" he asked. "Then let's get a license and make it true."

Alex shook her head. "No, Douglas, it wouldn't be right to you. You have plans. You told them to me, and I want you to carry them out."

"What good are plans when we are both being so unmercifully worried and plagued, darling? You know I love you—have loved you from the very first."

136

"I know," Alex told him, "and I love you, too, but we can't build our future on a lie, Douglas. Why not let it ride, and let Ridley do her worst. I'm not afraid— today, I'm not," she laughed wryly.

"But I am for you, Alex. And I suppose I shall have to explain something." He hesitated, and Alex saw that he was troubled and nervous. "Ridley swears she is going to—she declares that you are hiding something—that there is something in your past life that you want to remain hidden. I don't for one moment believe it but, darling, can she make trouble for you? Can she embarrass you? Don't say a word if you'd rather not, Alex. I am not in the least interested in your past—"

Alex Blair sat for a long moment, face downcast, gray eyes dark with pain, tender mouth pensive. At last she raised her head. "You would have to know sometime, Douglas," she almost whispered. "I should not be willing to marry you ever unless you knew. My brother Peter— darling Pete, spoiled, reckless and irresponsible—shot and killed his wife and then shot himself. It all happened the year I was eighteen. Peter had enlisted in the Army and— oh, I suppose it was bad company, the excitement of war— I don't really know just how it all happened, but it was in all the papers, some of it true but much of it grossly exaggerated. Pete was dead. Disgracefully dead, and the horror of it killed my grandfather, who brought us both up after our parents died."

Doctor Allen's hand on hers pressed sympathetically. "Never mind the rest, darling. You don't have to tell me anything. I love you."

"I want to tell it all, Douglas," the girl said slowly. "I was engaged at the time—to the only son of Valary's first citizen. He was afraid of the disgrace. His family was proud. So he went away. I sent him away, and he was glad to go. Don't, Douglas," as the young man swore under his breath. "I was young and flattered, but I know now that I never really loved him. So I left town. There was very little money after Grandfather died, and I went to stay with the sister of our family doctor. She sponsored me when I decided to become a nurse." She sighed deeply, then a smile of infinite sweetness brightened her somber face for a moment. "That is the complete story of my life, Douglas. Do you mind?"

Douglas Allen leaned forward. "Could I kiss you right here and now, Alex?" he asked recklessly, and she saw that his eyes were moist. "Would it cause a scandal, darling, and would they put us out?"

"I don't care if they call out the police or Ellen Ridley, Douglas," Alex said with equal recklessness, and lifted her face for his kiss.

There was a soft murmur of applause from an interested waitress somewhere far down the room, but it meant nothing to the two at the corner table.

"Is there something else?" the waitress asked, her eyes twinkling in amusement. "But I don't suppose there is."

Alex smiled and blushed, and Douglas Allen laughed aloud. "We had a delightful tea, Miss," he told her gratefully. "And we'll be back again. Ready, darling?"

They drove back to the hospital through the pouring spring rain, and when he parked before the side entrance, he asked softly, "Still not afraid of Ridley, Alex?"

"Still brave, Douglas," she answered. "But please be careful, dear. I believe she is quite ruthless."

Alex went into the lower hall and up the stairs to the third floor without seeing anything of Ellen Ridley. She opened the door to the passageway and hurried along its dim length and reached the nurses' section without meeting anyone. In her room, however, she found the night superintendent, apparently quite at home, reading one of her magazines.

"Hello!" she said coolly when Alex entered. 'You certainly choose delightful weather for your rendezvous, Blair!"

"Do you think so?" Alex retorted, feeling her anger rising, and determined to keep her temper, and not to let this woman see that she was annoyed.

"I saw you come in a moment ago," Ellen Ridley went on. "How is it that you and Doug dare flaunt Marie's precious rules so flagrantly? Don't tell me you think I took any stock in that wild tale of a secret marriage between you two, Blair." She laughed stridently. "I'm not quite a fool, my dear."

"Aren't you?" Alex asked blandly, although her gray eyes were black with anger. "And may I ask just what you are doing in my room, Miss Ridley?"

"Oh, I just dropped in to let you know that I'm aware

138

of your little game and intend quashing it when I decide the proper time has arrived. You'll never marry Douglas Allen, Blair—not after he hears some of the things I mean to tell him about your anything but stainless past." She stood up and started for the door, her cold blue gaze on the slender girl who merely stared at her in wonder that anyone so hateful could be related to their adored Chief. "Well?" Ridley asked. "Haven't you anything to say?"

"Well what?" Alex asked.

With a stifled imprecation the other went out and slammed the door, while Alex dropped weakly into the nearest chair. Had she done wrong in refusing to be friends with Ridley? Why was it that she held so persistently to the idea that the Chief's granddaughter was untrustworthy? It wasn't like her to be suspicious. She had felt from the very first that Ridley didn't like her. But, she acknowledged frankly, she had no tangible proof of her enmity other than gossip, and the fact that few of the staff spoke well of her. Why then, did she persist in treating the night superintendent as an enemy? Was it because of Douglas Allen—the fact that he feared her malice not for himself, as for what she might do to the girl he loved? Alex rose to her feet and paced the room unhappily. She was by no means proud of herself. Somehow a sense of guilt weighed heavily on her heart.

"I don't care if Ann does think her malicious and hateful," she told herself. "I can't help it if she and Douglas are at swords point. I am not going to be unfriendly any longer. Somehow I can't dispel the feeling that the girl is unhappy, and why shouldn't she be when almost everyone in the hospital dislikes her? When I meet Ellen Ridley next, I shall attempt to be pleasant. Maybe by so doing I shall be able to get rid of this feeling of dread. At least I can try. If she really meant it when she offered me her friendship, then it should not be too hard." She felt much better after this decision and hummed contentedly as she changed into a fresh uniform before going down to dinner.

CHAPTER SIXTEEN

IT WAS SEVERAL days, however, before Alex found the opportunity to put her plan into practice, for Ellen Ridley appeared to avoid her. When they did meet, Alex's smile was friendly, and after two or three such encounters, the night superintendent smiled briefly in return.

"Don't tell me you and Ridley have buried the hatchet," Doctor Allen said after seeing the exchange of smiles. "That girl is simply biding her time. I firmly believe she still means mischief. I don't trust her."

"Don't you think perhaps we have all been mistaken in the Chief's granddaughter, Douglas?" Alex asked. "Granted she has been spoiled and has an inflated idea of her importance here at Haddon, still I can't shake off the feeling that the girl isn't happy. How could she be when everyone is against her? We haven't been very kind to her, Douglas. Now have we? Let's try being friendly for a change, giving her a chance. It might work."

Doctor Allen shook his head at her, his smile tender. "You're an incorrigible sentimentalist, Alex," he told her, his ardent gaze assuring her that whatever she suggested was his pleasure to accept. "Perhaps you are right, although—"

"Don't argue with me, Douglas," Alex laughed. She hurried down the long corridor to the elevator, knowing that his eyes were following her. She looked back when she pressed the button and waved, smiling happily at his answering salute.

There was a new patient in 417—a Mrs. Ferris, wealthy widow and prominent club woman. She had been brought to the hospital an hour before, suffering from a coronary thrombosis—an occlusion which it was feared would prove fatal. She was a tall, spare woman, whose handsome face was often seen in local and out-of-town papers. Now as she lay propped up in bed, her breath short, her face ravaged by pain, she had the appearance of being a fighter. Her lips were set firmly, and from time to time she murmured that she would soon feel better, it was just an attack that would pass. Alex admired her spirit, and watched her closely.

"I'm not yet ready to die, Nurse," she said, when the pain had lessened a bit. "There are so many things I must do before going home. It isn't that I love life so much as that I like to finish what I begin. It isn't right to leave work only half done. Is it? Stay and talk to me, my dear," she urged. "You look sensible and as if you knew your business." It was all said haltingly, the shortness of breath making the going hard. "I told Doctor Mathews I would not have specials. I want you. Do you understand?"

"I understand, Mrs. Ferris," Alex assured her, wondering if she was to be allowed to remain on duty here.

The resident came and went. The Chief dropped in once or twice during the night, and it wasn't until the room became gray with the early morning light that the patient fell asleep—a quiet, restful, almost natural sleep. Doctor Hammond nodded approval.

"She may pull out of this, Blair," he said almost doubtfully. "But we must watch her closely. Another attack like this will finish her. The woman has an astonishing constitution. She is seventy-one. Would you believe it?"

Alex shook her head. "She is a beautiful seventy-one, Doctor," she murmured, "and a wonderful one. All the things she does. All the plans she has. The world needs women like her."

"It certainly does," the resident agreed. "But somehow they are the ones who go first it seems." He left the room, and Alex watched the quiet breathing of the patient for a moment. Did it fluctuate? Was it more labored? She found the pulse, and after a moment saw that needed badly or not, Mrs. Ferris's earthly work was finished for all time. She saw Doctor Hammond leave a room farther down the hall and motioned to him.

"It is all over, Doctor," she said softly. "She went in her sleep."

"Perhaps it is well," the resident murmured. "She would have hated invalidism and dependence on others. Death is by no means the worst thing that can come to a person, Blair. Take it easy, girl. Your relief will be along in a few minutes." He patted her shoulder, and smiled sympathetically for Alex was close to tears. She had fought every moment. Fought as her patient fought. And lost.

Alex was feeling depressed when she returned to her room some time later. She had eaten a light meal and gone directly to bed, where she lay and tried desperately to sleep. It was not at all usual for her to allow the events of her working hours to effect her to the extent of causing her to lose necessary slumber, but Mrs. Ferris had fought so bravely and was so determined to recover, that Alex

141

was especially unhappy at her death. She experienced a feeling of defeat it was difficult for her to shake off.

Morning was well advanced when at last she slept, and was awakened by her alarm which sounded at one o'clock, its usual time. Simultaneously came a gentle knock on her door. She lay still and called "come in," expecting to see the housemother who had very often lately urged her to breakfast in the kitchen downstairs. But it was Ann Mordock who entered. Ann was dressed for the street and held in her hand an airmail letter.

"This came just a few minutes ago, Alex," she said handing the missive to her friend. "Arizona? Air mail and in a masculine hand, too. The plot thickens. What are you keeping from me—your pal?"

Alex turned the letter over and over in her hand, her face puzzled. "I don't know who can be writing me from Arizona, Ann," she said. "I don't know anyone out there."

"It would probably be an excellent idea to open it and find out," Ann advised. "You may have an unrecognized admirer, or even an unknown rich uncle who is leaving you a few million. Open it, Alex," she urged, "I'm curious."

Alex slipped a nail file along the envelope and drew out a single sheet of paper—a long sheet covered with writing. Her eyes darted to the signature at the bottom of the page. "Richard Grandon!" she exclaimed in surprise. "The pneumonia patient in 513. I didn't know he was in Arizona, Ann. He had an infected right lung. A fine looking young man, and a most impatient and trying one to his nurses."

"What does he say?" Ann wanted to know. "Why is he writing to you, or is it none of my business? Of course he fell in love with you, or thought he did."

"Nonsense!" Alex replied. "He did nothing of the sort. Listen, I'll read it to you. Although—no—o, on second thought I don't think I shall. It is sort of—"

"Sentimental?" her friend teased. "Don't mind me, Alex," she went on. "I can take it. Read it," she urged. "I haven't heard a real, honest to goodness love letter in ages."

"No?" Alex asked skeptically. "Aren't Jim's epistles sentimental? Don't tell me that for I won't believe it." She folded the letter and slipped it into its envelope.

"I think you're mean," Ann chided.

"All right then," Alex said resignedly. "I'll read it to you. Though actually I did very little. But listen."

" 'Dear Miss Blair,

" 'You will probably be surprised to hear from me, but I felt an urge to let you know how very much you helped me while I was a patient in Haddon.

" 'You will remember that I told you I had never had much religious training—my home wasn't a religious one, and I had never felt the necessity of asking or expecting divine help. But I want to tell you that I followed your advice, and have found not only peace but help as well. My moments of quiet receptiveness have brought me something far more precious and beneficial than either medicine or change of climate could possibly have accomplished without it.

" 'I am sure you will be interested in knowing that my doctors tell me I am responding satisfactorily, and that I should be able to return east in another six or seven months, at which time I hope to see you again.

" 'I must add that I can never thank you enough for *showing me the way*. Frankly, Miss Blair, I think you are the finest girl I have ever known, I mean it.

" 'Gratefully yours,
(Signed) Richard Grandon.' "

Ann sat for a moment, her face pensive. "That was a wonderful letter, Alex," she said at last. "It is so seldom a person's advice is followed or a nurse's care appreciated. I don't think I have ever heard sweeter praise. If that letter had come to me I believe I should frame it, Alex. Now tell me just what it was you did for him—'showed him the way,' he wrote. Just what was the formula you recommended, Alex?"

Somewhat hesitantly Alex told of her experience in cases such as young Grandon's where the patient was depressed and even frightened—a condition that so often delays recovery and is detrimental to physical as well as mental health.

"It is really a recipe, Ann. An application of mental therapy. A relaxing of tense muscles and taut nerves. A time of quiet so that the soul may reach out to Infinity for the help and strength that is ever waiting in such abundance." She laughed a bit self-consciously. "I sound like an exhorter, don't I, but I have seen the almost miraculous healings that have resulted from this 'waiting on the Lord' as my grandfather used to call it. He always contended that we are so busy asking, demanding, complaining that we never give God a chance to speak to us. Be that as it may, Ann, I firmly believe that a quiet time each day in the midst of the hectic rush of life will pay big dividends in health, physically as well as mentally and spiritually. I have seen it proved time and again so I know." She paused and looked almost apologetically at her friend.

Ann Mordock reached her hand to that of Alex and pressed it closely. "You're sweet, Alex," she said softly. "I wish I had your faith—your rare gift of helpfulness. Haddon Memorial is extremely fortunate in having you a member of its staff, and I am lucky to call you my friend."

"Aren't we the sentimental pair!" Alex said to change the subject back to normal. "I'm lucky to be here, Ann, and happy that you are my friend. Now, darling, tell me something about Esther Knowles in 526. They tell me she has an intestinal ulcer. Is she very ill? Is it a case for surgery? And isn't she the girl who is to be married some time next month, or is it in June?"

"Doctor Widmer, the family physician, seems to be doubtful that it is an ulcer, and I believe she is having x-rays this afternoon. The Chief, however, has no doubts about the matter although Widmer insists on x-rays, so x-rays are what she is submitting to right now. The girl has lost considerable blood and will probably have to have transfusions."

"No surgery, Ann?"

"I don't know. Undoubtedly it will depend largely on what the x-rays show. Bartlett told me she had been given the first pint of barium and they were waiting to see the results. I hope she recovers in time for the wedding, Alex. It is to be a gala occasion from all accounts. Her people are wealthy, you know, and she is the only child— daughter, anyway."

"Isn't she quite young for an ulcer, Ann," Alex asked.

"It would seem so, although I think I should take the Chief's diagnosis rather than that of a mere physician if it were I, Alex. But the girl is scared to death."

"You mean afraid they will operate? Well, I happen to know of a case—oh, it was several years ago—six or seven—where a young girl was operated for an ulcer in the duodenum. She was, perhaps, twenty-three at the time and the ulcer had closed off the outlet to the stomach. She was in excruciating pain most of the time. Well, the operation was very successful. A new outlet was made into the stomach, she was hospitalized for three weeks or a month, and returned home perfectly well. Anyway, she married six months later and now has twin boys—and no ulcer. I, too, believe the Chief may be right. I should trust him."

"You may have the opportunity of helping this patient. Alex," Ann said. "If an operation is indicated you can give her courage. She will probably need it. I'm so glad you are to stay on in the west wing, darling. You're a rare nurse. An inspiration to us all. Even Ridley seems to have changed. Or hadn't you noticed?"

Alex nodded. "Do you know, Ann, I believe some of the fault was ours. I mean the staff's. The fact that she was the Chief's granddaughter predisposed us to consider her bossy and egotistical. We looked for things to criticize. If she was friendly we felt she was patronizing. And when she appeared cool, we thought she was putting us in our place, showing how superior she was. Her position wasn't easy."

"Okay, okay," Ann interrupted, "so her position wasn't easy, and just where does that place us? What are we to do to show our friendship?"

Alex laughed at the other's rueful face. "I'm not doing much of anything—just not aggravating her by being stiff and unfriendly. Perhaps I have been the worst offender, and I am thoroughly ashamed. She may not be willing to forgive and forget, but I intend meeting her more than halfway and treating her with consideration. I hope it works. If it doesn't I shall have done my part anyway, and will no longer feel guilty."

"I see what you mean, Alex," Ann murmured. "And I will back you up in the campaign to humanize the Chief's misunderstood granddaughter." Her tone was skeptical, but Alex felt sure she meant what she said.

It was when they went down to dinner later in the afternoon that Ann added a proviso to her declaration of belief in her friend's campaign. "Suppose the lady refuses our proffered hand of friendship, Alex," she offered. "Suppose she scoffs at our delayed acceptance of her place in the scheme of things. What then? Oh, don't misunderstand me, Alex. I'm all for burying the hatchet—if she doesn't sneak back to dig it up after our backs are turned."

Alex laughed. "You're funny, Ann. This isn't a political campaign. There is no axe to grind. We are merely going to treat her as we treat the rest of the staff."

"All right," Ann demurred. "How would it be if I went up to her and poked her in the ribs and cried, 'Hi, Ellen! Come on up to my room tomorrow afternoon and we'll have a jolly time.'"

"After all, she is our superior, Ann," Alex pointed out, grinning at the other's clowning.

"That I will never concede, Alex Blair," her friend countered. "Her position is a mere tentative one. It was made for her because she refused to consider the position of nurse or even of supervisor. It wasn't because she knew more than the rest of us. Oh, she had college training, but just the same that doesn't necessarily prove she is a better nurse. No, my pet, she is night superintendent merely because of her relationship to the Chief, and don't make any mistake about it."

"Granted you may be right, Ann," Alex said, "but as long as she is night superintendent, she is our superior."

"All right. All right," Ann agreed, "you win. Now let the curtain rise and here's hoping the performance will prove that you are correct as always, and we have all been suspicious, disagreeable and uncooperative brats."

Both nurses were laughing as they entered the dining room and were met with smiles and friendly glances from the others at the long table. Even Ellen Ridley looked less reserved and haughty, and Ann nudged her friend as they took their seats.

"I believe your particular brand of alchemy is working, Alex," she whispered. "It's in the very air we breath. More power to you!"

CHAPTER SEVENTEEN

ESTHER KNOWLES was a badly frightened girl. Doctor Mathews had won the decision, and there would be an operation early next morning. The day supervisor had advised the general duty nurses, Nora Craig in particular, to give her as much of their time as was possible, and Ann Mordock offered the same advice to the nurses on night duty. Bailey and Morrison were sure they could manage with, perhaps, the aid of a student nurse. They felt exceedingly sorry for the patient, and were sure that if it were at all possible Alex would succeed in dispelling the gloom that hung like a black cloud over 526. Now as she entered the room, Alex smiled encouragement at the girl in the narrow hospital bed, and was rewarded by an almost imperceptible wave of a hand in return. Alex drew near to the bed.

"I am Alex Blair, Miss Knowles," she said quietly "And I am going to spend the night or most of it here with you. Do you feel just a little more comfortable, or is the pain still severe?"

The girl's wide blue eyes filled with sudden tears. She caught Alex's hand and clung tenaciously. "I'm ashamed of being such a baby, Miss Blair," she said. "But I'm scared to death. Do you think it might be cancer instead of ulcer?"

"Not at all alike," Alex told her comfortingly. "Not a chance in the world. You can trust Doctor Mathews. Trust him completely. If he considers surgery indicated then it is best. Tomorrow at this time it will all be in the past, and you will be back here in bed and well on the way to complete recovery. I knew a girl who had the very same thing—only worse because she had suffered longer. You were wise to come as soon as the first symptoms appeared. The girl I knew had suffered for three years before hospitalization. But within six months after the operation she married and is a proud mother of twin boys. There! Please don't worry. Don't be scared. And we are all going to pull hard for you. What would you like to do tonight, or are you to have callers? Sometimes callers are considered unadvisable before an operation. However, you are young and strong, and Doctor Mathews could easily have given orders to let you have visitors. Anyway, I shall be right here and if I think you are getting tired, I can see that they leave."

"Bill wanted to come but I wouldn't let him. I—I look so terrible. So washed out and—"

"I think you are wise and very brave, my dear," Alex told her. "Better have him come tomorrow when you are rested and relieved. How about your family? Are they coming?"

"Mother and Dad wanted to, but I advised against it. Mother would go to pieces, and Daddy would insist on camping out on my doormat. You see, Miss Blair," she smiled, "I'm the pride of Dad's heart, so I told him I would be all right, and for them to stay right at home and pray for me. They will, too. I mean pray for me."

"I'm sure they will," Alex agreed. "You are such a lucky girl to have your parents."

"Haven't you?"

"Both my parents died when I was a tiny child, and my grandfather brought my brother and me up. Now I am all alone in the world."

"How awful!" the girl whispered, then brightened for a moment. "But you won't be all alone for long. Are you in love? Engaged?" And as Alex blushed rosily, she laughed almost gleefully. "You are! you are!" she cried. "I'm so glad for now we have something in common. Let's talk about our men, Miss Blair—Alex. May I call you Alex? I hate anything as impersonal as 'Nurse.' "

"Of course call me Alex if you like, and I shall call you Esther. Tell me about your Bill. Is he wonderful, handsome, madly in love? And when and where is the wedding to be? Do you expect to live here in Haddon? And what does your Bill do?"

"Oh, I like you, Alex," the girl said, a faint color in her pale cheeks. "This is fun!"

The door opened, and the night superintendent entered to stand beside Alex. She looked down at the patient with interest. Her slim fingers picked up the wrist outside the coverlet, and for a long moment there was silence and a quiet that seemed almost ominous in the room. At last she replaced the hand and turned to Alex.

"I suggest quiet and relaxation at this time, Blair," she said coolly. "Did Doctor Widmer leave medication of any sort?" And at Alex's reply that none was indicated in the report or mentioned on her chart, she went on, still impersonally, "I shall get in touch with Doctor Widmer or, failing that, with our Doctor Hammond. Grandfather is resting at this time and should not be disturbed." She turned and left the room. Alex was surprised. Ann had said nothing to her about special medications or the necessity for quiet. On the other hand she had advised trying to take the patient's mind off the subject of the approaching operation.

"Don't pay any attention to her," Esther said shortly. "I shall do exactly as I please. She isn't my nurse. Doctor Widmer didn't tell me to be quiet. He said I wasn't to eat anything, and that after my bath in the morning I was to have a hypo. She can just go peddle her papers, Alex. We're going to talk about our men. Draw up that easy chair and be comfortable. I am not the least bit sleepy, and I don't intend even doing any napping."

"But sleep will do you good, Esther," Alex told her, "help you relax."

"I slept off and on all day, and I don't need any more right now. I shall probably sleep most of tomorrow, too. People generally do after an operation. Forget that woman's orders, Alex. They don't mean a thing to me."

She did doze occasionally, however, and each time she was annoyed that drowsiness had overtaken her and spoiled her plans. But she smiled approvingly when her eager gaze encountered the friendly smile of her nurse.

"Hello!" Alex greeted her.

"It's so nice to find you here with me, Alex," she said. "Now let's talk some more."

Doctor Widmer made a visit soon after nine that evening, and Doctor Hammond stopped in several times during the night. Alex wondered if Douglas would come in, too, but remembered that it was his evening off, and he had planned to make a flying visit to Centralia where a colleague was speaking before the Rotary Club of that city. Doctor Widmer appeared somewhat gruff at first, but very soon relaxed and pronounced himself well pleased with Doctor Mathews' diagnosis and entirely in favor of surgery. Doctor Hammond joked with both patient and nurse, and on his last visit which occurred around three in the morning presented Esther with a small, fuzzy white panda.

"It's a good luck animal, my dear," he said. "You hold it tight when you take that ride to the operating room, and be sure you bring him back with you. His name is Bill after a certain other Bill who thinks a great deal of an especially lovely young lady I could mention if I'd a mind to."

"Bill!" whispered Esther her eyes enormous in he white face. "Is he here, Doctor? Where is he?"

"Oh, behaving like a husband already, my dear," Doctor Hammond told her. "Visitors are never encouraged to remain all night in Haddon Memorial, you know, but what do you think that headstrong young rascal has done? He coaxed and wheeled the Chief. Played upon his heartstrings, pleaded, cajoled and bribed that sentimental old man until he turned over his private office to him. And that is where the rogue is spending the night. I tell you, girls, love is a wonderul thing. Hang onto his talisman, my dear. It's potent."

The patient's eyes were shining as she whispered childishly to the small furry panda. "He's sweet and I love him!" After that, she slept until nearly five o'clock when Alex was preparing to leave. "Why can't you stay with me, Alex?" she demanded. "I want you here when I leave and when I come back. Why can't you?"

And Alex whose eyes were heavy and whose tired body cried out for bed, smiled and assured her that she would see what she could do about it. Ann Mordock arrived, and the matter was put up to her, but Ann promptly vetoed the idea.

"Miss Blair has been on duty ten solid hours, Miss Knowles," she pointed out. "She must have her rest. She will be on duty again tonight at seven. Don't tell me you are nervous, my dear!"

"What do *you* think?" the girl demanded. "How do I know I shall come through the operation? People *do* die from operations you know."

"And you're the girl that brash young man in the Chief's office boasted to all and sundry as being the bravest, pluckiest, gamest, most courageous girl in the world! Is it possible?"

"Oh, go ahead, Alex," the patient grinned wryly. "Sleep the sleep of the just. You've been swell and I'm just a scared-cat. Don't let them move you to someone else tonight though. I need you. And," she said shyly, "I want you to meet my Bill. Wish me luck and—and pray for me, Alex."

Alex stooped over the bed and pressed her hands against the pale cheeks. "I shall, my dear," she promised.

"Don't be afraid, Esther. The Chief is a great surgeon. He'll take care of you, never fear."

"Honestly, Alex," Ann muttered as they moved down the long hall to the elevator, "what has she to be scared of? The Chief has done that sort of job hundreds of times."

"But never on her before, Ann," Alex pointed out.

"Of course. But where's all the grit that poor sap downstairs has been telling the world is her chief characteristic? Love sure is blind. If she marries the lug she will have to face many worse things than a simple operation as this will undoubtedly turn out to be. Let us hope he won't find her out."

"Don't be so unfeeling, Ann," Alex chided. "Remember, it makes a world of difference whose ox is gored. From where you stand the operation appears to be a simple affair. It isn't your body that is going under the knife. I sympathize with her. She is brave and plucky and sweet and good even if she is frightened. I have a notion I should be scared, too, if it were I."

"There you go," her friend muttered resignedly. "Well, here's hoping everything works out according to Hoyle, or rather Mathews, and that her young man gets to see her before many hours. Why, they are even serving his breakfast here. Imagine! I bet if it was anyone else, the Chief would never have turned over his precious office to him."

"He would if he were handled right," Alex laughed. "One has to know how to handle the Chief."

"Humph!" was Ann's only answer, as she poured cream into her coffee.

When Alex went on duty that night she found not only Esther Knowles' Bill in her room, but her parents as well.

"I had trouble getting rid of the others," Craig, the day nurse complained. "They claimed to be her cousins, her bridesmaids, her pals, and everything under the sun. But out they went just the same. I hated to do it but I had strict orders from Hammond, Doc Widmer, and even Halliday that visitors were to be kept out. I asked about the family and her fiance and they shook their collective heads, which I took to mean they were okay. I doubt if anything short of a police force could have kept that Bill Cameron out. Lucky gal to be the object of so much adoration."

Alex liked the Knowles family and young Cameron as

151

well. The patient, though pale and wan and still a bit groggy, looked infinitely better to the nurse's trained eyes. It was very quiet. No talking. Just quiet, loving attendance.

"My blood matches, Miss Blair," Bill told her confidentially. "I've been typed, and it's my blood they are going to use. She's going to be all right, isn't she?" he asked anxiously. He looked tired, and Alex felt sure that he had not slept at all during the long anxious night of waiting.

"I'm sure she will. Much better than before, when she gets over this. Of course she will have to be careful for a time, but I'm sure with her youth and basically strong constitution she will soon be well. You are a lucky young man, you know. Esther is sweet."

"And don't I know it," he replied fatuously.

Mr. Knowles seemed unable to take his eyes from his daughter's face, while the mother sat close to the bed, one of the girl's hands clasped in her own. It was a lovely picture, and a little stab of envy shot through Alex's heart. How wonderful to be one of a family! Suddenly she knew a nostalgic longing for Valary, the friends of her girlhood, the fine old home where she had spent a carefree, happy childhood.

"I'm going back," she told herself. And for the first time in the years of her absence there was not bitterness or dread in the thought.

Esther Knowles was right in her prediction that she would probably sleep most of the day and night following the operation and she did just that, to waken just before Alex went off duty. Her eyes were clear, her color slightly better, and her smile the sweetest Alex had ever seen.

"I'm better, Alex!" she said almost happily. "I told Bill and the family about you, and they will probably want to adopt you after I'm married. Are you leaving right now? Why didn't you wake me? We didn't get half talked out. I have so much to tell you. And I want to hear all about your man." She laughed a mere bubble of mirth. "Come to think of it I did all the talking, didn't I? I don't even know your man's name, Alex. What is it? I bet he's a doctor. Darn it!" she muttered peevishly, "here comes your relief. But I shall give you the third degree tonight. Good-bye now. See you tonight!"

Nora Craig approached the bed, her hands bearing the paraphernalia for the patient's morning bath, and Alex left.

CHAPTER EIGHTEEN

RAIN FELL MOST of the night, but when Alex went off duty at five the next morning the east was beginning to glow with soft colors, and the world was filled with the scent of growing things. Somehow the strain and stress of the past weeks and months seemed to have lessened, and Alex prepared for bed in a state of peace with all her world. She set her clock for one, and slept soundly throughout the morning. With the whirring of her alarm she stirred, stretched lazily for a moment, then slipped out of bed. The early spring sun was warm, and she stood before her open window breathing deeply of the perfumed, rain-washed air. She flung her arms wide. How glorious to be alive on this bright spring day!

There was a faint knock on her door, and she caught up a robe and called, "Come in!" Mrs. Martin, the house-mother, put her head into the room.

"I came to invite you to breakfast in my kitchen, Alex," she smiled. "I have been baking most of the morning and have fresh rolls, molasses cookies, the kind you especially like, and everything is ready when you are."

Alex laughed. "You spoil me, Mrs. Martin," she chided, "but do you know, I love it. I'll hurry with my bath and dressing, and will be there in fifteen minutes or less."

The housemother left, and Alex joined her in the immaculate kitchen in less than the time she had promised. She was dressed for the street and dropped coat and beret on the nearest chair before taking her place at the table which had been laid for one. She ate hungrily, and Mrs. Martin beamed happily. This girl seemed to ease the lonely ache in her heart. Her one child—a girl of Alex's age—had died in one of the air raids that had devastated such a large part of London.

"I suppose you are going to take advantage of this lovely spring afternoon to go for a walk in the country?" she surmised, as Alex drank the last of her coffee.

Alex nodded. "I've been dreaming of the glen along the outlet, Mrs. Martin," she said. "The first violets grow

153

there, you know, and if one is lucky there is mountain laurel, too. Last year I found a great bunch and brought it back to the hospital. The children loved it. Remember?"

"I remember," Mrs. Martin said. Then added somewhat dubiously, "But it is sure to be very wet I'm afraid. Don't forget that it rained all day yesterday and most of the night. Perhaps tomorrow would be better for the glen, Alex."

"Oh, I'm neither sugar nor salt," the girl assured her. "I always wear heavy walking shoes when I go hiking. And don't forget, Mrs. Martin, that I never take cold. Don't worry about me. This is just the day for the glen. Just the day to find special treasures."

And so Alex walked the short two miles to the small park with its artificial lake or pond, its really beautifully landscaped grounds, and its winding paths that wandered for miles through the thickly wooded glen. Birds never sang more gloriously. The air was never fresher. The foliage never a more tender green. She strolled along the path that circled the pond, and came upon Ellen Ridley dreamily watching the swans floating lazily on the quiet surface of the little lake. But this time Alex felt no resentment toward the older nurse. She called a gay greeting, but didn't pause. Ellen Ridley barely replied. Her eyes never left the water before her. Alex walked on and was soon out of sight. How lovely it was! She began to sing softly, then stopped in amazement. When had she felt this upsurge of spirits before? Not since Valary days before tragedy struck. That was before she had discovered what real love was. Before she had met Douglas—darling Douglas! Her heart bounded in ecstasy, and she took little dancing steps and laughed aloud. Oh, it was wonderful to be young and in love on a glorious spring day!

A stifled scream of terror from a few feet ahead hastened her steps, and she saw through the trees the small clearing and the bench set close to the deep, swiftly flowing water of the outlet. The head of a child of about four appeared above the water for a moment, and without a sound as quickly disappeared. Alex shed her coat and slipped down the sheer embankment into the water, muddy and swollen from the recent rain. The outlet was waist deep in this spot and just now made dangerous by debris brought down from the hills above. An excruciating

154

pain in her ankle made her cry out for a moment, but her searching hands caught and held the child's shoulder, and she tugged hard to free him from the entangling branches of the submerged trees which were holding them both fast in their clutches. With difficulty she managed to lift the child's head above the water and saw that he was unconscious. There was a long scratch on one cheek, and his head lolled to one side as if the clavicle was broken. But he was alive. Of that Alex was sure. She tried desperately to free herself from the tree and reach the bank which a moment before had been so close—well within her reach.

"Bobby! Bobby!" someone called stridently. A young woman came running along the path and gave a shriek of terror when she saw the two in the water. Scarcely pausing, she ran screaming down the path toward the park. In a matter of seconds, that seemed hours to Alex, Ellen Ridley appeared followed by the still screaming woman.

"Hold on, Alex!" Ellen Ridley called, throwing herself flat on the bank of the stream and extending both hands toward Alex.

"I'm caught. There's a tree or something in here that is holding me down. Can you take the baby?"

"Sure," the other agreed. "Hand him up if you can."

"I—I'm afraid we're both caught. I'll—I'll try."

"For heaven's sake don't faint, Alex Blair!" Ellen Ridley cried sharply. "Are you hurt? Oh, Alex, don't faint. Please don't faint! I can't reach you. I'm coming in, too. You," she commanded the screaming woman who was evidently the child's nurse, "you run to the nearest house and call Haddon Memorial Hospital. Tell them to send Doctor Allen with the ambulance at once! Scoot! And for mercy's sake shut up!" Something in Ellen Ridley's voice made the woman obey, and she dashed off.

Ellen Ridley managed to liberate the boy, and deftly swung him onto the bank. He still clutched his plastic duck.

"Is he—is he all right?" Alex gasped.

"Sure," Ellen Ridley said. "After we get you out, we'll turn him over and help him get rid of the water he swallowed. More scared than hurt, I would say." As she talked she tore at the slimy branches of the submerged tree, and at last managed to free Alex's ankle. "Don't you dare faint, Alex Blair!" she scolded over and over. "You'll

155

be out in a jiffy, now. You *are* hurt, Alex, but don't faint. Don't you dare faint! There, there!" she encouraged. "Try to grab that boulder. Here I'll boost you—up you go. Don't worry about me," as Alex urged her to get out and leave her, "I'm like a cat and can wriggle out of any situation. Doug should be here any minute now if that fool girl—"

She paused as a young woman, evidently the boy's mother, accompanied by an elderly man, panted to a stop beside the unconscious boy, the man muttering incoherently, and the woman gathering the child close. They appeared quite unaware of the two young women still in the muddy swirling water of the outlet.

"Suppose you give us a hand here," Ellen Ridley said crisply. "This girl saved your child's life and was badly hurt doing so. Your hand, please," she demanded of the man who looked up in astonishment. Ridley was sure he was the woman's father, and appeared almost feeble, but he reached his hands to Alex, who clenched her teeth and gasped as he pulled with all his scant strength. With Ridley's help from behind she was shoved and pulled to the bank where she promtply lost consciousness. Her legs were torn and bleeding, her ankle swollen, one shoulder sagged, and an arm hung limp. Her face was scratched and she was very wet and muddy.

Ellen Ridley's touch was amazingly gentle as she wiped the blood and mud from Alex's white face. The pad, pad of running feet brought her upright. Doctor Allen and the ambulance driver raced along the path bearing a stretcher.

Bobby's mother cried, "He's hurt! My boy's hurt!" She raised a tragic face to the two men. But Douglas Allen had eyes for but one person. He went to his knees beside the unconscious Alex. Ellen Ridley attended to the child, and soon his eyes opened and he gagged satisfactorily. At once he began to cry lustily.

"Donal' pulled me in!" he screamed. "Bad, bad Donal'," and with an angry gesture he tossed the toy into the water where it floated serenely down the stream while the youngster, fascinated into quiet, watched as it disappeared from view. "Don-al', Don-al', you come back here!" he screamed but Donal' was completely out of sight.

"I imagine his collarbone is broken," Ridley explained to the child's mother. "We'll take him to the hospital and fix him up in short order. Here, take the boy, too, Doctor," she said, as Alex was being borne along the path on the stretcher. "I'll carry him."

"You will do nothing of the sort," the mother cried indignantly. "I will take him home and send for our own family doctor."

"As you please," Ellen Ridley told her. "He will be all right. I should suggest, however, that this glen is scarcely the proper place for a four-year-old's play-ground."

"He probably ran away from Sadie, his nurse," the grandfather explained as the mother, her son in her arms, went along the trail and out of sight. "Come on over to the house and into dry clothes, Miss," he went on almost apologetically. "My daughter is upset. I hope—"

"Think nothing of it," Ellen Ridley answered, wringing the water from her skirt. She smiled wryly because the stretcher had left without her, but the smile left her face when she heard someone calling her name. "Yes!" she answered, "I'm coming," and ran toward the summons.

She climbed into the front seat beside the driver and pulled her wet coat around her.

"You're sure dampish, Miss Ridley," the driver of the ambulance told her superfluously. "What happened?"

Ellen explained, making light of her part in the rescue, and the man who had been loudest in condemnation of the Chief's granddaughter, surprised himself by almost liking her. To be sure her face was dirty, her blond hair hung in untidy strings, and her once immaculate suit was torn, muddy, and very, very wet. But there was something appealing about her. Something almost gallant in the way she refused to adopt the role of heroine. But it was plain to be seen that she had saved the lives of both the boy and the nurse.

There was quite a furor at Haddon Memorial Hospital when news spread of Alex's heroic deed, and it wasn't until hours later, although Alex kept repeating the fact of Ellen's brave and—under the circumstances—almost superhuman rescue, that they knew of the part Ellen Ridley had played in the saving of both victims. Doctor Mathews, however, made it clear that he was extremely proud of his granddaughter. He recounted the spectacular rescue to any and all who would listen. Not that he belittled Alex's part in it, but he pointed out the fact that both would have undoubtedly drowned if his girl hadn't risked her own life to save them. As it was, Alex suffered from badly lacerated legs, a sprained ankle, a dislocated shoulder, and multiple cuts and bruises, not to mention shock. It was two days later, however, that pneumonia developed, and for days her life was almost despaired of. The staff talked in whispers. And Douglas Allen became haggard and hollow-eyed.

"Weren't you surprised when Ridley demanded the right to nurse Blair, Morrison?" Bailey muttered. "Somehow I can't seem to take it in. What has happened to her, and how is it that she can quit her job as night superintendent to go back to nursing? How is it that Halliday would let her do that without making an issue of it? Things have certainly changed around here, Morrison, and I can't understand it. I hope you remembered Blair in your prayers as your promised," she went on.

"Sure I did, and still do," the younger nurse said indignantly. "I keep my promises, Bailey, and what's more I have a hunch our prayers will be answered. We need Blair, Bailey, and I know darned well Doctor Allen needs her. The poor lug is sunk. But do you know," she went on her face pensive, "I've got an idea Ridley's a changed person. Maybe she's got religion, or maybe she's decided to take that Bruce we've heard about lately. Do you think maybe she has?"

Bailey smiled and patted the other's shoulder. "Could be either one," she conceded, "but somehow I have a notion that she has suddenly discovered one can catch more flies with molasses than with vinegar, as the old saying has it. She's clever, that one. Well, it's all to the good whatever the cause of the change, and I'm all for it."

"You've lost weight," Alex told the night superintendent—just now her special nurse—one bright morning late in May. The Chief's granddaughter was arranging to advantage the flowers that even now arrived daily from friends, ex-patients, and members of the staff. "I'm sure it is due to your wonderful nursing that I am here now. I was so terribly tired, you know. But I think you need a vacation, Ellen. You look as if you could stand a good long one. I don't think it is at all necessary that I have a special any longer."

"I shall stay on this case until you are able to sit up, at least, Miss Blair," the other replied firmly. "Oh, Alex, what a fool—what a beast I have been! I am so terribly ashamed of myself! Sometimes I think I have been the victim of a dual personality. I wanted to be friends. You were always so good. So sweet. I adored you, and yet I seemed possessed to be hateful and jealous. I don't know what got into me."

"It's all over and past now, Ellen," Alex said soothingly. "You saved my life twice. I shall never forget that and believe me, my dear, I am not at all proud of my own actions in the past where you are concerned. I could have been more friendly—less critical and more cooperative. Maybe I was jealous, too. It makes me happy to know that we are really and truly friends at last, Ellen. You are a grand girl, and I love you."

The other sighed. "I'm afraid Doctor Allen isn't so generous, Alex," she said ruefully. "He's cold and stiff to me. Barely civil. And your pal, Ann Mordock, too. She objected to my nursing you. Did you know that?" Her voice thickened for a moment. "I had the impression she was afraid I should harm you. It hurt terribly. How could I have allowed myself to gain such a rotten reputation, Alex?" The blue eyes, usually so cool and impersonal, filled with tears. "Grandfather has been sweet since your accident. He used to get angry with me—wanted to ship me back home, but now he seems to understand and to excuse my bad behavior. He's a wonderful man, Alex. I love him dearly." She pressed a hand to her head for a moment, then laughed shakily. "They say confession is good for the soul. Perhaps I shall feel better now. I'm a little tired."

And it was that same night that the Chief of Staff ordered his repentant granddaughter to bed in the room next to the one Alex had occupied for the weeks of her illness. Ellen suffered a complete nervous collapse, during which time she relived many of the unhappy moments of her recent weeks—the misunderstanding with the staff, the quarrel with Douglas Allen, the struggle in the dark swirling waters of the muddy outlet, and through it all ran a constant call for Bruce. And when one evening Bruce was ushered into her room, she seemed to sense his presence there and grew quiet. That night was the turning point in her illness, and from the moment when he took her thin hands in his and begged her to get well and come home—that he needed her—she improved rapidly.

But late June was rioting over the Haddon countryside by the time she was well enough to accompany him on short drives. Doctor Allen was still inclined to be a bit skeptical at the change in his once arch enemy, but Alex was so happy and relieved at the turn of events that he had perforce to accept the situation, and gradually the old animosity was forgotten. After all, he had Ellen Ridley to thank for giving Alex to him.

Bruce lingered on in Haddon. He seemed reluctant to leave. He confided to Alex that he hoped Ellen would marry him before he left—marry him from her grandfather's house. The Chief seemed in favor, and only Ellen demurred. Haddon Memorial was short of nurses. She was needed badly, and confided to Alex that she wanted to stay on and prove to the others— especially to Halliday—that she really was a fine and understanding nurse.

"And believe it or not," she murmured ruefully, "I want them to miss me when I leave, not because they are glad to see the last of me, but because I was a good nurse." And Alex understood and sympathized. Her own stay at the hospital was growing short, for Douglas Allen had decided to become a general practitioner, a family doctor in a small community upstate. Doctor Hammond called him a short-sighted fool refusing a chance at a big city practice, but the young surgeon still held fast to his three-fold dream—medicine, surgery, and research. Space in which to work, to grow, to make a life with the girl he loved.

Alex knew he was hitching his professional wagon to an almost inaccessible star, but she loved him for it and felt that if anyone could make a success of the venture, her Doctor Douglas Allen could. She would be there working beside him every step of the way.

THE END